Fina Casalderrey
DOVE
AND
CUT THROAT

Published in 2014 by
SMALL STATIONS PRESS
20 Dimitar Manov Street, 1408 Sofia, Bulgaria
You can order books and contact the publisher at
www.smallstations.com

This book was first published in the Galician language as *A Pomba e o Degolado* by Edicións Xerais de Galicia (Vigo, 2007). The series GALICIAN WAVE: The Way of Fiction exists to showcase the best of Galician young adult fiction in English.

More information about Fina Casalderrey can be found on the author's website, fina.casalderrey.com.

This work received a grant from the General Secretariat of Culture of the Ministry of Culture, Education and University Planning of the Xunta de Galicia in the call for translation grants of the year 2013.

Esta obra recibiu unha axuda da Secretaría Xeral de Cultura da Consellería de Cultura, Educación e Ordenación Universitaria da Xunta de Galicia na convocatoria de axudas para a tradución do ano 2013.

ISBN 978-954-384-029-8

Fina
Casalderrey

Dove
and
Cut Throat

Translated from Galician by **Jonathan Dunne**

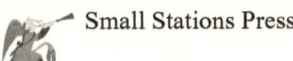 Small Stations Press

To my pupils at the secondary school Salvador Moreno in Marín.
To Manolo and Cruz for letting me inside their birdhouse.
And to you, of course...

'Yeah, I like birds, so what? Just because I have a thing about them, don't believe it, that's another story. There's stuff that won't let me sleep, I'm warning you. Recently I've started getting up at night, going to the kitchen, grabbing the sharpest knife I can find and then heading straight for the exit with the aim of sticking the knife in the chest of whoever has hurt me at some point in my life. I have to be restrained because I'm out of my mind. There are times I even have to be tied with ropes until I calm down, just in case I succumb to another fit… I want you to know that accepting my friendship means belonging to a high-risk group because, I'm telling you, when I fly off the handle…'

I had to intimidate them somehow. School had turned into a place where I was failing on a daily basis. Every morning, when I went in, I looked at those walls and felt like running away, as if from fire. Putting up with all the abuse day after day was pretty hard, and there was no way I was going to bother my mother with all that nonsense. I quickly realized that at school it was your appearance that mattered.

When they found out I had a bird in my rucksack, I couldn't let them spread that rumour about me being a softie, I couldn't stand being humiliated all over again, so I used the same methods as Raúl Pernas and his gang. I put on a show. As a result of my outburst, there were fewer jokes, that's for sure. As for Halima, she deserved an explanation, but where am I supposed to begin? Do I tell her, 'The point is I'm a kind of swift, living in the air all the time, and if I fall to the ground, I need a helping hand to help me take flight again,' or say, 'It's just I'm tired of playing the autistic parrot my grandpa saved'?

That parrot from Patagonia was never in its right mind. Maybe that's why it never wanted to leave the house. It was always moulting and had permanent bald patches behind its head. It was a bad-tempered bird that didn't know the right way to go about asking for things. Maybe it was because of its chronic illness that grandpa adopted it for his own private field hospital.

The bird was spoiled and had a free licence to enter the house, wander about the kitchen, go wherever it liked. I only had to sit down to breakfast for it to demand a ration of cake with shouts that sounded like insults. We called it Captain Flint, after Long John Silver's parrot.

Shortly before dying, and despite its lamentable state, that greedy, autistic parrot caught sight of my breakfast bowl and immediately demanded something sweet with deafening screeches. Then it followed me to the bathroom and stood stock-still on the rail. It reminded me of Edgar Allan Poe's 'The Raven', I could hear its 'Nevermore' as it extracted a sad smile from my fantasies that burned inside my chest. It was like a dry leaf waiting for a breeze to send it down into the abyss. I drew the curtain and, at that precise moment, it fell to the ground. It started shrinking, shrinking… just like a balloon losing all of its air. It put on a scarf, as Grandpa Guillerme would say, and that was the end of that. I suffered terribly!

Should I explain all of this to Halima? I haven't even dared ask her the meaning of what she wrote in my notebook.

There's only one girl I can talk to openly. That's Dove I chat to on the Internet. Until today, Dove was the sea, the water in all its immensity, the beyond, freedom... I imagined her walking on the surface of the waves, her hair adorned with seaweed. She's clever, she knows how to say the right thing. 'In a way you're lucky,' she told me when I was suffering because of grandpa, 'I never knew my grandparents.' That made me think... Dove was the friendly voice that reached me through the computer's loudspeaker, but now I'm supposed to meet her in person, and I don't know what's wrong with me.

Halima... Halima's more tangible, she's the seashore where the foam sends kisses, the salt of the sea perhaps...

2

The salt, the sea…

The social sciences teacher had given us a headline: '130 immigrants caught in Almería in three boats'. We had to come up with a story on the theme if we wanted an extra mark in our final evaluation. At that stage, I'd already stopped studying so hard, and this was the only chance I had of passing. I ignored the fact I felt so ridiculous and started reading the story Dove from the Internet had given me, just as I'd printed it out. It was written in the first person, in the voice of a woman. As soon as I realized, I felt grotesque, but I managed to keep on going until the end.

SHADOWS AT SEA

I was young and full of hope. I knew nothing about the conditions I would have to travel in, or about endless queues, day and night, in front of the consulate to obtain a good-conduct certificate, or about walls without a soul, or about Moroccans breaking their backs working over here… I had no idea about the days without food and work of many men and women who, seated on the parapet of despair, had not been allowed to do illegal seasonal work for refusing to pay the foreman thirty euros so he would 'miraculously' find them a place. As far as my ignorance went, I didn't even know how to swim.

That 25 January, my mother woke me in the middle of the night. 'Put this on.' She gave me an anorak and the only shoes I had: some old trainers I'd received in good condition and never knew where they came from. 'Get up, get up quickly,' her voice was mysterious, but I sensed what was going on. We were finally leaving for Spain, where our financial difficulties would come to an end, and our adventure begin. Mother was prepared to work hard, and I would attend university. The effort to save for the crossing had finally borne fruit. We might even find my father, from whom we'd heard nothing after he left Chaouen. In a happy frame of mind, I attempted to picture a face in my memory that had been eaten up by time. I wish in the same way I could erase my mother's lost look in the ocean, or her wounded voice repeating my name, using up the last breath she had. That terrible scene has remained inside me like a damaged vital organ.

A man was waiting for us at the front door, to take us north in a van. As far as Nador, next to Melilla. There were more people there, in the same situation. He dropped us off as you would drop off some merchandise that nobody paid any attention to for several days, I can't remember how many. All I know is that I was sorry to have wolfed down that tuna sandwich and that apple. A day later, I was trying to locate the core when my mother secretly gave me a piece of her sandwich; she'd kept it for me from the evening before.

I don't want to talk about what happened during the days that followed until another man finally appeared and took charge of us and the other fortunate few who'd handed over their money in order to give free rein to their dreams.

In hopeful silence, we followed him to the coast. Nobody dared speak. My mother simply held me close. Two men arrived on a rubber dinghy and gestured to us to get quickly on board. The men on land made sure who went first. There were more than fifty of us! It struck me as impossible that we'd all fit in that boat. They counted us... sixty!

And so, clustered together like a bunch of grapes, we set out for the unknown. In complete darkness, we had to avoid any security cameras that might be controlling the perimeter separating Morocco from Spain. I felt uncomfortable, but content. The clouds helped us along the first part of our journey by keeping the moon hidden. The lights on the coast were also gradually swallowed up by the distance. In spite of the darkness, the sky for us was filled with lights. The air smelled of sea, of plenty, of paradise; but also of fear and insecurity. The two men who were rowing cut the water with unusual slowness. A cloud emptied itself over the boat. I felt myself getting wet and shuddered.

Many nights before making the crossing, I'd thought about the voyage and not been able to sleep. I'd even heard the sound of the waves, just as I was hearing them at that moment. Nobody else could sleep. There was only one man whose head kept drooping. A woman next to him had her eyes more open than anybody. She seemed too tired even to sleep and had a baby wrapped in her arms. 'That baby's not leaving any memories behind,' I thought and felt envious.

Shortly afterwards, the man started snoring like a bagpipe. If he'd known a few hours later he'd be dead, he wouldn't have been able to sleep a wink.

The sea was calm. The boat moved slowly, like a nutshell.

I stayed awake the first hour, getting used to looking in the dark. The feet of the wind shone across the sea. We stared at each other, a numerous, improvised family chewing over the hours.

'Play at spotting the first star,' my mother whispered honeyed words to me and, in that hollow silence, I gazed at the sky. Finally, I saw it, and then another, and another... The clouds fell behind, and the moon used this opportunity to sink into the sea. 'That's the Little Bear,' I again felt the warm breath of her voice in my hair. I lifted my head up and caught sight of an enormous firmament, and felt well...

I don't know if it was the spluttering of the engine or a shiver down my spine that woke me. We were far away from the coast, and the noise from the engine no longer sounded out of place. It was getting light. Everybody remained where they were, concern etched on their weary features. We were like a painting by El Greco, an artist I'd recently discovered. The whole of my body ached, I needed to stretch a bit, but there was no space.

The sea grew choppy, and the enormous hood of my mother's anorak kept slapping my face like a colourless seagull. The boat resisted the solemn beating of the waves, leaning over more and more. A wave crashed into us and, in an effort to avoid it, some people got to their feet. The dinghy listed dangerously. 'Nobody move!' a sudden shout made itself heard above the voice of the sea, and we turned into statues. That was when I noticed the two men responsible for the crossing were the only ones wearing life jackets.

The cold, the roar of the waves... I suddenly felt an irresistible urge to pee. I was sitting on my mother's legs, but even so I had to go. I felt her icy hands stroking my face in stark contrast to the warm liquid running down my thighs. 'Not long to go,' I seemed to understand from the kiss she deposited on the back of my neck.

'We're reaching Motril, on the Granada coast. As soon as I give the word, each to his own!' shouted the one who always gave orders.

'That wasn't the agreement!' protested the man who'd been snoring like a drone.

Other men and women contributed to his protest. It started with an outbreak of words, but soon people began gesticulating and moving about. I could see the disaster coming. That man, the only one who had some knowledge of the language spoken in the country we were going to, as I later found out, fell into the water. Others tried to rescue him, but the Zodiac was listing violently... I watched him getting left behind, splashing about in the icy water. It was like having your leg cut off. Everybody's gaze became silent and acquired a salty sheen.

'We have to move away from the coast?' the other man in charge of the journey, who up until then hadn't spoken, was talking on a mobile.

The Maritime Safety Agency and the Civil Guard were searching the coast. We headed back out to sea. It was a serious blow to our hopes. The dinghy turned into an enormous disappointment. The sun appeared in the east, but it wasn't exactly welcomed like a king.

We floated at sea for a whole day, waiting for night to descend, so we could attempt another disembarkation. Just water and sky for hours, along with the unbearable stench of vomit.

From time to time, the waves imitated a storm, and the dinghy rose and fell like a typhoon. It was impossible not to get wet. The water was so cold it acted like an intravenous injection of ice, with an immediate effect on our temples and nose. My mother hugged me closely, though I felt her slacken every now and then.

We saw fish, but nobody spoke about them. There weren't even any comments when a wave slowly brought us the bulk of a drowned man with violet skin and entrails devoured by the monsters of the sea. It didn't look like the man who'd fallen off the boat.

Silence and anxiety, only ever broken by the crying of the baby. The woman fed it from her breast, and the baby calmed down. I was thirsty, hungry and cold, and my lips were dry. My mouth filled with saliva. Once again, I wished I was that baby. My stomach protested. My mother heard its groan and kissed me on the back of my neck, as if to say, 'Don't worry, as soon as we set foot on dry land, there'll be a succulent couscous waiting for us.' But I felt she was tense, glancing at the horizon with uncertainty.

Under cover of night, we again approached the coast. We were weak and exhausted from cold and hunger. The moon made no concessions, showing itself quite clearly.

Again, a black dot on the sea coming towards us. 'At last, we're being rescued,' I thought and gave thanks to heaven. We weren't used to the sea, and I was so afraid…

'A coastal patrol!' shouted one of the raftsmen.

'Into the water, you can almost walk there by now!' ordered the other.

I can't be sure about anything after that. The sea swallowed me completely. For a few seconds, I moved my arms in a desperate attempt to regain the surface. And, through the whistling wind, I heard the clear, agonizing cry of my mother repeating my name in the middle of other shouts. That's the last I can remember.

When I came to, I was shivering under a pile of blankets.

I carried on hearing my mother's broken voice for many days. After that, her shouts turned into prayers: 'Come on, eat up. You have to fight if you want your dreams to come true. Promise me you will.'

I realize now I was one of the lucky ones. Natalia and Manuel couldn't do more for me, they give me everything. Even so, whenever I hear news about boats going down in the strait, my blood boils out of a feeling of impotence and a sense of anxiety I need to get out of me.

Which is why I'm writing this.

When I finished reading, I noticed an exaggerated silence. Raúl Pernas had been expelled that day and, without him, Héctor Solla didn't dare stick his nose in. Feeling confused, I met Halima's moist gaze and felt an electric shock run through my body. She was moved and managed to transmit this feeling.

I think the teacher was impressed as well, judging by the expression on her face, though all she said was 'Number?' so she could give me a mark. I shuddered as if I'd been dealt a blow, but it was Halima who disturbed me most when she leaned over my desk and whispered:

'How well you read!'

My ears went bright red. I wasn't honest, I didn't dare confess I'd been given the story by a friend from the Internet.

I was about to tell her so, but in the end I lost my nerve. Last year, it would have been easier, after Christmas we sat next to each other. Now the classes are over, what am I going to do? Grandpa was right: 'Nostalgia is like a suit that's smaller than it should be and squeezes your chest.'

It's 25 June already...

3

Today, 25 June, I dreamed of a voice I'd never heard before, a face I'd never seen. I got anxious.

It was Dove who took the initiative of arranging to meet. I have the sensation my stomach grew smaller the moment she made the proposal: 'At eleven, next to the newsagent's in the Alameda.' Does that mean she's from Marín? How come we never talked about this? As the hour approaches, my doubts beat more and more strongly in my fingers, as if they were infected. We humans have lots in common with birds: we also are born without defences.

Would you look at me! I think I used too much hair gel, I can't stand these bouncy curls. A few drops of Hugo Boss... I'm going to clean my glasses. I used to blame my father's irresponsibility for my short-sightedness and other misfortunes, but maybe there's no need to search for people to blame and Dove is right: 'Forget about that, you can't go losing the crypt of your dreams. If they wake you up from a dream, you die.' She likes to invent alarming theories. She and the birds were the best therapy I could have had to endure and even overcome recent events. Until today, when we were chatting, I could show myself as I am, without adopting any disguises. Why did she arrange to meet? Things were fine as they were.

I'm never able to see danger coming. Even a blackbird can sense when a bird of prey is on the lookout, and yet I can't withdraw to safety even when I receive a warning from a friend. At the time of the Swiss girl, Curro tried to warn me: 'Watch out because she's leading you on.' But I didn't pay any attention until I'd turned into a broken puppet.

Did I close the door properly? It's still early. I'll have to while away the time somewhere. How thin the moon is! It appears and disappears, playing at passing the minutes, just like me. It's not cold, I can't understand why there are so few people in the street.

This is how my grandpa must have felt when his first boat drifted out to sea with a crack in the bow. Yeah, that's right. I'm a castaway. Life flashes past me in a moment. Perhaps it's true we are what our memory has chosen. There are stories that are full of meaning, even though I didn't understand the reason when I was small. They're memories that become sharper than when the events happened, as if I'd read about them in a book.

I was in control of the remote for the first time ever! I pressed number three, and *The Simpsons* came on. It was a strange lunch, not because everybody was quiet, that had happened a lot recently, but because I had the remote and no one seemed to mind.

Suddenly, as if her chair was on fire, my mother jumped up.

'I have to go out,' she said with a little too much emphasis.

Davinia went with her, slamming the door.

I sensed something was wrong. I didn't say anything. Father made some coffee and disappeared to his room. I turned off the telly and followed him. His movements had become very fast.

'Are you going away?'

Tula barked, reinforcing my question. I went around in circles while the dog wagged its tail, waiting for an answer. There wasn't one. The doors of the wardrobe, the chest of drawers, bedside tables, everything had been opened at once, creating a kind of chaos that was greater than usual before a trip. Two gigantic suitcases covered the blue duvet. Father seemed to be practising the role of some burglar for a casting and shoved everything in with complete abandon. I supposed his trip wasn't planned and it would depend on how quickly he could organize his luggage whether or not he got to the airport on time. Tula breathed energetically, as if responsible for making all this fuss.

When I saw him pack his collection of fountain pens and that Panama hat he only ever wore in summer, with Christmas just around the corner, I thought it must be a very strange trip he was going on and insisted:

'Father, where are you going?'

He didn't even flinch, but carried on stuffing all kinds of unusual objects into the suitcases: a silver trophy, a guide to exotic trees, books he'd already read... He even included that book on Hindu mythology I liked so much, which had a bird with a human's head and arms on the cover. 'The Garuda is half eagle, half man, it hatched from an egg that was left to incubate for more than five hundred years,' he'd told me. He used it to teach me to read.

'Why are you taking that?'

He didn't answer, and I realized I'd suddenly become invisible.

That 29 November was the last time I saw my father at home, excluding the lightning visit he paid me several weeks later.

I found it strange that he should have taken those things he wouldn't let anyone touch, which turned him into my favourite hero. Add to that the fact he worked at a disco. 'You have no aspirations,' mother had said accusingly. My concept of aspirations had something to do with the way we breathe. Mother didn't understand the advantages of having a father on the door at a disco. All Davinia's friends were envious of her purely because of that. My sister, at the age of fifteen, could go to afternoon sessions without having to show her ID and, as soon as I turned fifteen, I'd be able to do the same.

'Shut it, midget' was the answer I got when I tried to persuade my father to take me with him.

Midget…

The times I'd stood in front of the mirror, waiting for the earth to swallow me up, I felt so anxious. It was Curro who unwittingly helped me overcome this complex. He's older than me, and yet he seemed younger.

It was St Andrew's Eve and, since my father wasn't paying me any attention, I went back to the sitting room to look for clues that would help clarify things. I was still in charge of the remote, master of the world. I again heard the front door banging louder than was necessary. I ran across to the window. Father, with Tula on a lead, was putting the suitcases in the car. Shortly after that, his Ford disappeared in the direction of Calvo Sotelo Street, and I couldn't see him any more.

I guessed all this mystery had something to do with preparations for my sixth birthday party. I felt calmer. On other occasions, all those serious faces had simply been to hide a magnificent surprise. The first came when my mother returned home and told me to put on my anorak.

'Where are we going?'

She didn't want to explain. I understood perfectly, a surprise is a surprise. Out we went.

Several cold, practically invisible raindrops began to scratch my face.

I didn't ask her any more questions. We were obviously in a hurry, we didn't even have time to respond to our neighbours' greetings. We went down to Ourense Avenue, it was all I could do to keep up.

We finally reached the park. There was the surprise! Autumn had turned the ground into a yellow lake. Mother knew there was about to be a flood. She could always foretell the rain. How often had she waited for me at the school gates with an umbrella in her hand and at precisely that moment the sky had begun to bucket it down!

That afternoon's surprise game consisted in slowly stepping on the leaves of oaks: yellow ones, brown ones, muddy ones, broken ones… We went over them again and again. The rain became more intense. The point was to step on all of them without leaving any behind, without an umbrella, without talking, without looking at each other and without starting to laugh. She was so serious!

A dark raincloud drained the sky of its colour and poured the water of the whole universe on top of our heads. Mother, who'd never allowed me to play in the rain and got hysterical whenever something like that happened, continued concentrating on the game, her eyes fixed on the ground. The pleasure of puddles was within my reach, and I started jumping in them with my Wellington boots until I could hear the water singing inside. I would have loved to say, 'Thanks, mother, this is the best present ever!' But I wasn't able to break the magic of that silent, mysterious tangle. I could hear the laughter of the water banging on the leaves and didn't want to hold back any longer. With a sense of elation, I let go of her hand and ran through the park with my arms open wide. The world was mine! I jumped in puddles and flew like a vulture, which feels the power of having no enemies that will dare eat it. My hair stuck to my neck and brow, my nose was like a drainpipe. I followed my mother around, even though she couldn't see me, since she too had given me the present of invisibility.

The lights in the park began to tinge the evening with a golden glow. That was when I realized the magic of invisibility and rain had vanished.

'André, are you mad?' shouted mother reproachfully.

She took me by the hand and started talking nonsense. The game had most definitely come to an end.

Back at home she forced me straight into the shower. The water burned terribly. I still had to drink some honeyed milk, which scorched my throat and made me retch. I managed two gulps and got into bed. My mother's hair was still wet, and she still had those red eyes from lunchtime. I was trembling, but reassured her:

'Don't worry, mother. Playing with the water was the best birthday present of my life.'

She gave me a hug and a strange kiss, keeping her lips

pressed against my cheek for several seconds. Then she left my room without giving me time to ask about my father's unexpected journey. All I wanted now was to get warm.

I came down with one hell of a cold! I didn't go to school for almost two weeks and (I counted them) I didn't see my father for twenty days. That was a lot of days...

4

That was a lot of days without pocket money…

Davinia protested and said her pocket money had been frozen. I imagined it as a block of ice. Mine had disappeared as well, but I wasn't particularly aware of the gravity of the situation.

Circumstances could not have been more unfavourable until, one evening, someone rang the front-door bell. I looked through the peephole and saw a man with a beard. I didn't open, as I'd been told not to. The bell kept ringing, and I ended up turning into the little kid from the fairy tale.

'Who is it?' I asked that sudden wolf.

'It's your father, André. Open up, I've come to see you.'

My father was back from his travels! I opened the door and flung myself around his neck. It was strange he hadn't brought any suitcases or used his own key, but then it was also unusual that he'd grown a beard, knowing my mother didn't like it very much. But this didn't worry me.

'Where have you been, father? Were you on an island?'

'Something like that… Didn't your mother explain?' he kept up the mystery.

I shook my head and carried on with my interrogation:

'What have you brought me?'

'Brought you? From where?'

'From your trip!' I was getting impatient.

'I haven't been on a trip. Your mother knows perfectly well

where I've been. She can tell you, that's why you're here. I've come to find out what you want for Christmas.'

That year, I was having a mental struggle with the idea of Father Christmas. I'd just heard it was my parents. Things started to fall into place: the imminent arrival of Christmas, my father with that beard… The mystery of his disappearance had a simple explanation: as my father, it was up to him to play the role of Father Christmas and, as was to be expected, my wishes would take precedence. I could reel them off to him in person! I took this to be the case and enumerated my unending list of presents. I asked him for everything I could remember from the advertisements, while my father savoured the last beer in the fridge.

He didn't stay longer than a couple of minutes. I understood perfectly. I gave him a kiss, and he left.

His trip consisted in journeying around the world! Now I realized why he'd taken clothes for all seasons. As for Tula, the fountain pens and the chess trophy, they were simply credentials he could use on his extraordinary mission. Besides, Tula couldn't spend many days without father. He was the one who'd brought the dog home and looked after it.

My mother soon arrived, and I went up to her without waiting for her to take off her coat.

'Father came to see me! He asked me what I wanted for Christmas.'

'I suppose he thinks he can buy you. Did he explain anything to you?'

'He said you would.'

I attributed her lack of enthusiasm to tiredness. In recent days, she had started behaving extravagantly. She would go and clean the houses of strangers, while ours was in a mess. She'd even become a fan of the lottery.

'So he wants me to explain it to you?'

'Don't worry, I already know!' I said uncontrollably.

Mother disappeared into the utility room. I soon heard the sound of the washing machine. She'd be mad if she didn't make the most of this opportunity to ask Father Christmas for a new machine, one without a block of wood supporting the rusty corner, one of those advertised on the telly.

Davinia arrived and, as was her custom, quickly entered her room and shut the door. I pleaded with her to open, I had some good news!

'I know why father's not at home! He came to see me today...'

'Oh, that idiot!'

She opened and let me in. My sister had no idea about the extraordinary privilege we enjoyed by virtue of being his closest relatives.

'This year, he's Father Christmas! That's why he had to leave...'

'Is that what that monster told you?'

'No! He just said I could ask for what I liked...'

'Did he not explain that he and mother are separated?'

'Separated?'

My sister replied like someone identifying the body of a drowned man, in a slow, ashen tone:

'That's right, André. He went off with some aunt.'

'Aunt Herminia?'

'Don't be stupid. He went to live with some woman he met at the disco. He had a fling with her one night and told

Uncle Ricardo. Uncle Ricardo told Aunt Eulalia. Aunt Eulalia informed mother, and that's when things got out of control.'

From everything she told me, all I understood was that we hadn't been to my uncle and aunt's house in Madrid for quite a while, despite the fact I used to love going.

In the days that followed, I found out that Davinia was wrong, Father Christmas had never been so generous! With a card from my father, I received the most amazing presents: a remote-control airplane, a Nintendo with three great games and the book about Garuda the birdman! It was like recovering a part of myself.

My mother and sister were never at home. I often used to eat at Grandma Neves'. I always liked that house. Grandma would stuff me full of sweets, and Grandpa Guillerme would show me his birds. He used to talk to me about the swift, how extraordinary this bird was that could sleep in the air. I was the only person in all the class who knew what a swift was. Grandpa also resolved the issue of our pocket money, going so far as to back-pay us, though I still couldn't appreciate the importance of this measure.

Were grandpa here now, he'd know how to raise the issue of my diabolical outbursts with Halima, and whether or not I should turn around and avoid meeting Dove.

Halima and Dove are two gazes that meet on a single coastline, port and starboard of a single vessel...

5

Port and starboard of a single vessel...

From Pedreiras to Arealonga, from Arealonga to Pedreiras, I went from house to house, keeping my balance as on the deck of a ship in the middle of the ocean. The little time my mother devoted to me she wasted by telling me off for leaving crumbs all over the sofa or forgetting to tidy my room. Davinia had turned into a problematic, autistic teenager, like the parrot from Patagonia, or at least that's what her tutor said to mother. I spent more and more time at my grandparents' house. Occasionally, my father would take me to see Celta play, though he never demanded anything of me.

To make matters worse, my mother had started going to night school, something I regarded as an eccentricity related to the birth of the stars or a sudden interest in nocturnal birds. I once hinted, only hinted, that I really wanted a computer. Her reaction was so bad I never brought up the subject again. She'd become absolutely incapable of showing any tenderness. 'Look at the end of your shoes. We can't be spending all this money...' Reproaches from dusk till dawn.

I got used to doing what she said without looking at her.

My father was something else. He opened my eyes to details I hadn't seen before. 'Do you realize how irresponsible your mother was on the eve of your sixth birthday?' I understood. That solemn soaking had almost cost me my life!

My mother was also to blame for Davinia's behaviour at school. 'It's your mother's fault for not standing up to her,' he explained. 'Do you realize? She comes and tells me about it. What does she want? Who's she living with?'

My father talked to me like a man. For him, it was important I was happy. My mother was always going on at me not to lose sight of my future. My future, something like the planet Mars.

My grandparents' restaurant offered menus to workers. On Sundays, the dining room would fill up with people playing board games. But the part that attracted me most was the backyard. That was like another planet. Under the vine, they would put tables which, in summer, remained busy until the early hours. Near the tables, there is still a small garden, separated from the rest by a hedge. That bit about the garden is just a manner of speaking, since there is only grass. I like it. At the far end, next to the oaks and pine trees that run alongside the wall, is the house of birds, the ones I just inherited directly. Which is why the restaurant is called *The Birdhouse*.

I'd like to show them to Halima. I could tell her all about the forty thousand species of finches that come from South America, with their stout beaks, and how naughty the parakeets are when they eat… Next to the feeders, another cannabis plant has sprung up. Which is how I know they sprout from seeds like lentils. It could be a real one, it has leaves with seven leaflets and is female. It's nice, but I'm going to pull it out. As Curro used to say, 'I've had enough of people atrophying my thoughts.' If he'd been with me, things would have turned out differently, but he ended up attending the school in Chan do Monte, I don't know why, after all Curro lived in the fishermen's quarter of Cañota and I was in Fonte do Oeste, near the cross. All I had to do was go up to Pedreiras do Medio, turn right, head over Sapos Alley, and I was there. I liked visiting. From Pozo das Pedreiras, you could see the sea, the boats, the port...

Curro was a real friend, he was the glass of water I went to whenever I felt thirsty. How mean I was! He's still offended with me.

I continue to be tormented by the memory of the day I took some marijuana leaves I'd picked in the garden to show the bullies in my year, with the naive hope this would enable them to leave me in peace.

'Hey, come and see what this girlie has brought us!'

I felt the veins in my head turning into liquid and everything inside me boiling like blood, but my impotence made me contain my fury. I kept quiet. Everybody was in awe of Raúl Pernas and his henchman, Héctor Solla.

That day was no different from the others. They made me go into the toilets and stuffed one of the leaves in my mouth.

'Swallow it, birdbrain, if you want us to leave you alone. Swallow it and keep your mouth shut. If you let on about this...'

So I swallowed. I don't know if it was already poisonous, or whether this was the result of my panicking, but the fact is I was in a terrible state for two days, unable to speak. I was going to die in silence, just like one of the birds.

The birds... I'll have to open their cages soon, the way grandpa used to. If I dare ask Halima to come, I'll tell her, 'The one coming out first is a canary, those are sparrows, there are two blackbirds...' until we can't count them any more and the sky above the yard fills with black spots dancing like pieces of ash. Some will return, others will disappear for ever, while we, holding hands as in the poster of a beautiful love movie, go fishing for dreams, inhaling each other's scent, as in that poem Dove sent me.

Dove... I feel an itching under my ribs...

6

When I remember what happened, I still feel an itching under my ribs…

My father, whistling, arrived at grandma's.

'I have a new flat in Pontevedra, André!'

'You bought one in Pontevedra!' I was overjoyed.

Curro had talked to me about new opportunities for having fun, and how there was a better chance of that in Pontevedra than in Marín. Father took me to the flat that day, it was just the two of us with Tula. Despite not seeing me for more than five years, the dog still recognized me and licked me all over my hands. 'It's like Odysseus' dog,' my father said. 'Ten years could go by, and it'd still recognize you.' I didn't know what he meant, but it sounded good.

There was a match between Barcelona and Real Madrid on the telly. We sat down, the three of us, in front of the screen. On a low table, which smelled new, there were peanuts and crisps. Party food! Tula lay down at my feet. 'Tula, be still.' And Tula obeyed.

My father had had a fight with me on the sofa and, once he'd managed to pin me down, I started shouting. Tula jumped on top of him, and he had to let go at once.

'That's right, Tula, you go ahead and defend him!'

If somebody wanted to do me harm, Tula was capable of biting them and tearing off a bit of flesh, despite being so small.

It was the best match I ever remember seeing. My father had become a fan of Barça, perhaps because my uncle Ricardo had given me a white shirt, which is why I supported Madrid. What a derby! We both managed to lose our voice.

A friend from Valencia had sent my father an enormous box of bangers and, as soon as the game was over, my father made the following suggestion:

'Come on then, let's let off a couple of rockets for each goal!'

'I'll let them off for the goals scored by my team!' I croaked.

'You bet!' he agreed, sounding just as hoarse as I was.

We opened the sitting-room window. It was mid-afternoon, an elephant cloud was floating across the sky. My father went first. He lit the fuse and sent a rocket flying into the sky with a loud crack. Then it was my turn. You had to hold on to the rocket with both fingers, without pressing too hard, so it could fly away as soon as it was lit. And that is what I did.

'How dare you make such a racket!' shouted a woman from the window opposite.

'I'm celebrating the goals with my son, madam!'

'With your son? How irresponsible!'

Tula was a bit on edge, and I ran to stroke it.

In the evening, father took me back to my grandparents'.

'Now you know, 5A. Think of the Fifth Amendment, and you won't forget,' he concluded.

I was almost twelve, and I understood. I couldn't stay yet. All he had was a bare sitting room and a folding bed. I'd got used to the new situation. Back then, I used to go round to Curro's a lot, though I also stayed at my grandparents'. We were rulers of a time that lumbered along like an elephant.

One day, I realized primary school was coming to an end and the following year I'd have to attend a secondary school different from Curro's. As if I sensed the distance that would spring up between us, I never left his side. He came looking for me with a dog he'd just adopted. It had been abandoned, like others he had. We went out. We liked to inspect the surroundings. We passed next to the cemetery, and that's when I heard a groan.

'Can you hear the sound of cheeping?'

Several chirps reached us from the top of a mausoleum.

Curro, who was more of a Spiderman than I was, offered to go and investigate. He clambered up the vertical wall until reaching a nest that had fallen on top of the tiles. The dog didn't stop barking.

'There's a baby!'

'Don't touch it!' I shouted. 'It might have ringworm, and your hair would fall out.'

Suddenly, the voice of a zombie boomed out from among the graves:

'Don't you have something else to do? Blasphemers!'

Curro almost broke a leg as he escaped. The nest went flying through the air. We ran like crazy through the priest's vegetable patch, dodging the potato stalks, crushing part of the crop, as we later found out from the priest himself, who turned out to be the zombie.

I couldn't get the chirps of that dying bird out of my head and ended up telling grandpa. We went back. The nest was on the ground, with the bird still inside. It didn't stop opening its mouth. Grandpa picked it up. I can tell a lot about someone from the way they pick up a bird. All I have to do is remember the way that brute, Héctor Solla, took a bird from me.

'It's a baby cut-throat finch. Poor little animal,' grandpa's hands were cupped so he could examine it.

'Has its throat been cut?'

'No, of course not! It's not visible yet, but you'll see how it comes out. It has a band of red feathers on the front of its neck, which is why it's called a cut throat. They're very easy to raise in captivity. They're resistant and fairly quiet.'

On arriving home, we put it in a cardboard box with a wool blanket in the bottom. Grandpa took an egg, beat it, immediately searched for a syringe in the drawer and filled it with that viscous, yellow liquid. Little by little, he poured the liquid down the bird's throat.

'Careful, you'll drown it!' I warned. But grandpa knew what he was doing.

I didn't leave the finch for the rest of that day. I learned it needed feeding every now and then. A week later, I was already preparing a mixture of egg and bread and placing small amounts in that beak that never wanted to close.

It was the happiest summer of my life…

7

That summer was the happiest, and most miserable, of my life. My mother spent the days working, studying or checking the lottery numbers, and I practically lived with my grandparents. I started seeing my father less.

The finch turned into my pet. I went so far as to give it a mythological name: Garuda, the birdman from my favourite book. As soon as it was strong enough, I took it out of the cardboard box. I thought it couldn't fly yet, but it quickly sought refuge under a kitchen cupboard. It stayed there for three days, without coming out. I carried on giving it food until it learned to trust me. I spent hours watching it. I wanted to see how the red colour on its neck appeared. I loved it more than my own life. After a few weeks, it was amazing, if I stayed the night at my grandparents', it would turn up next to my pillow early in the morning and wake me with a shrill squeak. It learned how to distinguish my whistle from others.

'Whew! Come here,' and it would land on my index finger.

It got used to wandering freely around the restaurant and soon became the star attraction. It didn't even flee when the windows were open. Once, we were in the kitchen, I held out my finger and said:

'Here, Garuda!'

It calculated badly and ended up in the frying pan used for

giving the rabbit a golden colour. Thank goodness the pan had been off the heat for a while! I took the bird out quickly and washed it with shampoo. It was trembling like a leaf when I dried it, I could feel it throbbing in my hand as if the whole of it was my heart. Garuda was partly me, in a way.

Grandma protested:

'This is no place for a bird! The grandson has as much sense as his grandpa! There's no help for either of you, it must have something to do with genetics.'

We laughed, knowing there was no intention in her words of modifying our behaviour.

There were always going to be frying pans in that kitchen, so I decided to take Garuda to Pedreiras. From Pituco de Arealonga to Fonte do Oeste – it's downhill – is twelve minutes walking. I took the path next to the cistern. I didn't even need a cage, the bird followed me like a puppy.

Davinia was listening to music when I arrived, and Garuda started chirping happily.

'Hey, a bird has come in!'

'It's mine.'

'How did it get here?'

'It came of its own free will.'

'Like I'm going to believe you.'

I doubt back then Davinia knew anything about the existence of a bird orphanage, or that grandpa used to play music by Luis Mariano or Carlos Cano for the birds, or that the customers gave them food when the tables were outside. Grandpa had devoted himself to this hobby since he was very young. When there were plenty of seeds, he would leave the doors of the cages open, so the strong ones could become independent if they wanted. 'We shouldn't restrict their freedom. However much we may love them, our worlds are different,' he used to say.

Davinia was out of touch with everything and found it difficult to believe that this bird would follow me of its own accord.

'You keep going on about this bird, why don't you open the window and see how much it loves you?'

I rose to the challenge. I opened the window in the sitting room a little and carried the bird on my finger. I gave it a push and said:

'It's OK, Garuda, you can go if you like.'

It flew outside, and I was upset at having helped it to escape.

'What did I tell you?'

I went over to the window in order to open it some more. At that precise moment, Garuda appeared, banging on the glass like a woodpecker. It was dying to come back in.

Davinia left after that, and I lay on the sofa with Garuda on my forefinger, thinking... I was an albatross gliding over the ocean, making the most of the winds, skimming the crest of the waves, slowly descending until I touched the foam, then heading into the wind, positioning my wings so I climbed slowly and splendidly, effortlessly zigzagging from side to side. I was exhausted.

When I awoke, Garuda wasn't there, and I started to look for it.

'Garuda?'

I called it, but it didn't appear. I whistled. Nothing. I realized the window in the sitting room was still half open and thought perhaps it had gone out through the gap and been unable to re-enter. I opened the window more and went back to the sofa. Just as I was about to sit down, I saw it. It had been crushed without giving a single whimper. I shivered as if a pain had shot through my body. I was the one who had crushed it. I picked it up. Its head was limp, it was clearly dead. I couldn't stop crying, holding Garuda to my chest.

This is how my mother found me when she came home. Her words of consolation only served to increase my suffering. She tried to make me feel better, but I just got more hysterical, until, in a sudden change of tactic, she gave me a slap on the face that rang out. She may have had a thousand defects, but my mother had never raised a hand against me. It struck me as so unfair! She snatched the bird from my hand with a disturbed expression I'd never seen on her before. I didn't know what she was going to do with it.

'Don't even think about eating it, you cannibal!' I needed to say something that would hurt her.

I decided to go and live with my father without telling anyone. After all, I'd been thinking about doing so for months. It wasn't yet six in the evening, my mother had disappeared, consumed by rage, and there was no reason for me, on the verge of turning twelve, to be afraid of going to the Alameda and catching a bus to Pontevedra. I knew my father's mobile number off by heart, so I phoned him and told him I was coming. When I arrived, there would be plenty of time to explain my decision to stay with him on a permanent basis.

On the bus, I sat next to the window and fixed my eyes on the glass: houses, trees, cars, Garuda… and my suppressed anger all filed past. I limited myself to biting my tongue in an attempt to hide the moisture dancing on my eyelashes from the other passengers.

I got off at the last stop, Galicia Square. I hesitated, not knowing which way to go. I wandered around for a while, feeling lost. All I could remember was the number of his flat, 5A – the Fifth Amendment! – but I couldn't find the building until I came across the town hall. There, I regained my sense of direction and walked straight to Ferreiros Street. When I arrived, my father wasn't at home, but he'd left the keys with the porter, just as we'd agreed.

'So you're Celestino's son, he never told me he had such a…' the porter was talkative, but I simply gave him a polite smile and got in the lift.

I emerged into the darkness of the fifth-floor landing, turned on the light and entered flat A. I immediately noticed a smell of varnish. The flat was unrecognizable, much more comfortable. The furniture was new, avant-garde in design, I liked it. I took a deep breath. I felt well here. I searched the flat and soon came to a room with two low beds, just the way I liked them. There was a huge chest of drawers, made with dark wood, the same as the beds, standing out against the orange wall, one of my favourite colours. I had an intimate corner just waiting for me! I burst out laughing. The room seemed to want to welcome me with sweet words only I could hear. I breathed in the happiness this surprise had caused me. I paid attention to the details: there were blinds, the same as in Curro's aunt's house, a desk…

What made me almost giddy with delight, however, was seeing a portable computer on the desk, I'd wanted one so much. At that precise moment, I betrayed Garuda's memory. If someone understood me, it was my father. I managed not to touch anything. I wanted to pretend I hadn't realized there was a splendid present waiting for me. I carried on with my inspection. In my father's bedroom was a double bed, together with an inbuilt wardrobe, just as in mine. I discovered a study, the kitchen, the sitting room, which looked bigger now… There were lots of books, and I traced the titles with my finger. There was one that caught my attention: *Bird That Fouls Its Own Nest*. I opened it and had a look, but it was just a series of articles that had nothing to do with what I'd expected. I put it back. The only thing that hadn't changed was the telly. I turned it on and sat down. It was difficult for me not to race to my bedroom and start playing on the computer, but I managed to restrain myself. That same evening, I'd ask my father to take me to fetch my belongings, I was absolutely convinced!

I don't know how much time passed. I was surprised by the sharp sound of the front-door bell. My father's voice was joined by other, unfamiliar voices. He obviously had visitors, and I ran to open the door.

'How's it going? Did you manage to find the flat all right?' he ruffled my hair.

I let it be understood that I had, I didn't think now was the time to reveal certain problems with my orientation. He was accompanied by a woman, and a young girl who looked at me sympathetically. I smiled back.

'Let me introduce you,' my father observed protocol. 'This is Raquel,' he gestured to the woman, who quickly gave me a kiss. 'This is Nuria. And this,' he ruffled my hair again, 'this is André. Come on then, you two, go and play.'

Where was I supposed to go with this little girl? Nuria pulled at me:

'Come with me. I've just been bought a computer with games on it.'

This sentence knocked me backwards more than if I'd drunk a pint of vodka in a single go and it had destroyed my liver. I don't know how long I put up with Nuria's childish comments. When I couldn't stand any more, I asked my father to take me home. My ribs hurt as if they'd received a pounding.

I didn't want dinner, nor did my mother ask where I'd been or tell me off. I got into bed, and she appeared next to me. She kneeled on the carpet, and her voice turned into breath:

'Are you still unhappy?' I listened with clenched fists, my heart beating like crazy. 'Don't you want to say anything, hey?' she waited for a few seconds and gave me a silent kiss. My hatred melted away at once. I realized if there was something my mother knew how to do well, it was kiss me. 'Forgive me for this afternoon, I was very nervous. I know what Garuda meant to you. You're my own Garuda, the only one. I dream of seeing you spread your wings and take off. I've just sat an exam and I think I'm going to pass. Then I won't have to be out so much of the time. I can help you with your homework.' As she spoke, she gave me intermittent kisses that acted like an anaesthetic and calmed the intrepid throbbing of my heart.

I became less talkative, imprisoned by my own fantasies. I preferred not to be noticed at school and actually managed to achieve this during the first month. I got more or less the same marks in tests as at my previous school. My mother bought us a computer. It wasn't portable, but it was a computer. I spent my free time waiting for Davinia to let me use it, doing my homework and going up the hill with Curro. I became more shy. I was even afraid of two bullies at school, Raúl Pernas and Héctor Solla.

'Hey, you, take your things and shift your arse,' demanded Raúl Pernas. 'I want to sit there. Get a move on.'

'Why don't you ask the teacher?' I suggested.

He responded by sweeping my notebook and other things on to the floor with the arrogance of a bullfighter at work, while I was the bull, striving to withstand the pain caused by the barbed darts.

After that... After that, there were lots of other occasions.

Having had lunch, I crossed over Pumariño on my way to Cañota. I'd arranged to meet Curro so we could climb up to Pituco after doing our homework. I was so lost in thought I didn't notice I was being followed until two boys came alongside me and pushed me against the wall of a building under construction. I felt my shoulders rubbing against the bricks. Perhaps I should have rebelled against them straight away, but my self-esteem was low after my meeting with my father, and I couldn't do anything. The rest all happened very quickly. They shoved me into the entrance of the building and carried on pushing me from wall to wall while calling me all sorts of names, the least hurtful of which was 'girlie'. Raúl Pernas then forced me to smoke that thing he smelled of sometimes in the toilets, when they wouldn't let you in, even though you were bursting to go. 'Come on, girlie, take a drag! Let's see if you can learn who decides where people sit, you birdbrain!' I can still hear their voices inside my head, even though Raúl Pernas has since left the school. I think he was transferred to one of those centres for problematic children.

With him gone, Héctor Solla has changed dramatically.

I felt sick and was only able to take three puffs. After that, one of them, I don't know who, started blowing smoke in my face, and my glasses got all steamed up. He then pushed me on to the other's feet.

'Clean them!' a loud shout rang out in my ear. I started wiping those muddy boots with my sleeve. 'Not like that, with your tongue,' the voice insisted.

I felt my glasses rubbing against the wet laces and a churning sensation inside my body. They then started kicking me on my shins, my back, my stomach… I had the impression my gut was about to burst and I began to throw up. They ran away. A feeling of rage gave me the courage to stand up and return home. Both my mother and Davinia were out. I put my rucksack down and went to wash my face. I entered the kitchen and saw the spaghetti was still warm. I served myself a helping, but didn't eat it. I flushed it down the toilet and used the brush to remove any traces of tomato sauce. I lay down on the sofa and closed myself inside a shell, like a cockle that has been disturbed.

My mother arrived and came up to me:

'How was school?'

'I got an A in maths,' was all I could say.

She fell silent. She sensed something was up.

That same evening, she sat on my bed and spoke to me:

'I'm not a perfect mother, I'm aware of that, but I couldn't bear the weight of making you unhappy because I didn't know how to raise you. The only person you've harmed is yourself. I understand you're going through a period when you want to experiment, but you don't have to try everything in order to learn the consequences or feel better.'

She had smelled the joint, she knew about such things. She showed me several laminated sheets with various products and their effects, and talked to me about alcohol, tobacco… and how easy it was to persuade someone of my age to progress from one substance to another. She explained to me cases of people in Marín that left me feeling amazed. And she did all of this with those eyes suffering from conjunctivitis that used to tear my soul apart. I guessed the truth of the matter would hurt her a lot more and decided to keep quiet. She made me promise I would never experiment with such products again, and I kept my promise.

8

My mother didn't keep her promise, she failed to pass that exam. There weren't many places, and there were lots of people who wanted to become auxiliary nurses, which is what she'd been studying at night to be. Her eyes acquired a permanent air of sadness. All she did was clean other people's homes, cover for somebody at the provincial hospital and stay in bed. She didn't even remember to play the lottery or tell us off for things. Our house was a drifting ship with a broken rudder.

My father didn't bother trying to buy me off with some kind of papal bull that allowed him to ignore my daily routine, and I decided not to visit his flat again. On one occasion, we coincided at my grandparents' house. Nuria was with him and, judging by the ease with which she moved around, I guessed it wasn't the first time she'd been there. He made as if to ruffle my hair, but I dodged his gesture and ran up the stairs. I was followed by that girl who stank of something horribly sweet and insisted on calling herself my sister.

'Hi there! What you doing?'

'What are *you* doing? I'm in my bedroom.'

'I came to see you.'

'Well, there's nothing for you here.'

'Yes, there is. You're my brother. That's why I'm going to sleep in the same room as you.'

At that moment, I again cursed my father. I cursed him twice: for having partnered me with a girl who was so clingy, who insisted on being loved, and for what she then showed me.

'Look,' she said, 'I found it in father's bedside table.'

I lifted the lid of that box and saw it contained a mixture of joints, pills and other rubbish I knew very little about, except for what my mother's intensive classes had taught me.

'You sure you found this in his room?' I felt as if I'd been driven through with a stake.

Nuria gazed at me with satisfaction. She hoped to buy my affection in return for sharing secrets. If her idea was to distance me definitively from my father, she certainly achieved this. I limited myself to addressing her in a softer tone:

'Listen, Nuria, you shouldn't touch this, so I'm going to keep it. And don't go rummaging through his things, unless you want to get him angry, understand? Now leave me alone.'

'Why don't you love me? I love you.'

This statement elicited a smile from me that lessened my desire to know whether she was my blood-sister or not. What did it really matter?

I hid the box, planning to ask my father for an explanation one day. It felt strange. I understood Curro's anxiety concerning his father's problems all the more clearly.

During that first year at secondary school, I came to the conclusion that life was a mire, with sweets scattered here and there that were increasingly difficult to get hold of.

Discovering my mother in some corner with her eternal conjunctivitis was very painful, just as painful as her wish to be perfect, always ready to blame herself for our mistakes and to burst into tears.

One afternoon, the front-door bell rang in an insistent, unfamiliar way. I was alone and had no choice but to open.

'Good afternoon, it's the police. Is this the home of Davinia Santomé Lobeira?' the one who appeared to be the boss spoke authoritatively.

'No… not here…' I lied, feeling afraid.

'Are you sure?' asked the other policeman.

I shook my head again, not daring to look them in the eye.

My cover-up didn't last long. They only had to stand guard at the entrance to our building, with a photograph they'd obtained thanks to the cameras of a large department store in Vigo, to catch her. It was like a scene from a film, in which my sister had unwittingly played the leading role. She'd swiped a few articles of designer-label clothing. What filled me with despair was the thought that Raúl Pernas and his gang might find out about it.

Strange things were happening at home, not just my sister's kleptomania, but also the fact that, while I began to understand my mother better, Davinia was growing apart. It killed me listening to them argue, without my mother defending herself. 'If you were the perfect mother you would have us believe, you'd know how to earn a living. If you're not, then you should never have left father. I hate you for not being cleverer!'

The same afternoon I received a visit from the police, the two of them came back from the police station. My mother had paid for the stolen items and got Davinia out of that mess.

This was the second time I became invisible. They shut themselves in Davinia's bedroom and talked and talked…

I decided that I was the one who had to change, I couldn't let things affect me so much. I started with school. Perhaps if I got lower marks, people would stop picking on me.

My sister also began to change. At weekends, she would go and look after my father's girlfriend's daughter in return for thirty euros an evening. Right now, she's studying psychology at the Open University, perhaps in an attempt to learn how to remain calm. She's certainly improved. She speaks to me differently: 'André, would you mind coming here for a moment?'

9

'André Santomé Lobeira, would you mind coming here for a moment?'

The school counsellor was one of the few people who knew my name. Even so, when she appeared in class at the hour of tutorials and I heard my full name, I got up, feeling terrified, and followed her without asking anything. I knew what this was about.

We went down the stairs, crossed the main corridor, passed in front of the teachers' room, the principal's office… I felt like I was on death row. We went back up the stairs on the other side and entered her office. I was fully aware only people who created problems ever crossed that threshold and I was in trouble. She asked me to sit opposite her, stared at me without blinking, and it was like being left naked inside an igloo. I grabbed hold of the chair so she wouldn't notice me trembling. It hadn't been me, but nor could I say the names of those who'd started all that nonsense.

'What is it, André? Do you have any idea how much you've changed recently? Do you realize she's probably going to have to take some time off due to depression?'

She meant the music teacher.

'She's not the only one,' I blurted out.

'I know, your mother was here yesterday.'

That was a low blow. I was a cornered fox and I fell silent, acted dead so I could escape. I knew I couldn't let on if I wanted to keep going; another beating like the one at the start of the year, and I wouldn't be here to talk about it. What should I say? Should I tell her how some of my classmates terrorized the rest of the class, me in particular, how they had it in for me and, if I spilled the beans, then I could go about preparing my coffin? Should I explain about the tests they subjected us to if we wanted them to leave us alone? 'Tomorrow at five a white car on such-and-such a street has to be burning...', 'There mustn't be a single shop with its windows intact on such-and-such a street...' and much worse things I would prefer to erase from my memory. Should I confess I have a kleptomaniac sister, a mother with a tendency to depression and a father who is a deserter? Should I tell her all of this? No way, that was my problem.

My mother had been at school the day before and not told me about it. I imagine the scene and still the blood rushes to my cheeks. She would have immediately burst into tears and confessed how miserable her life had become. I also found it difficult to cope with the break-up; you never think your parents' love could have an expiry date. It still hurts me now, but I learned to control myself.

'What is it, André? Let's see, you're a good boy, what happened with the music teacher?' the school counsellor insisted.

'Nothing.'

'What do you mean nothing? Do you think switching CDs so you can make fun of her is nothing?'

She rebuked me, but gave me a chance to reply. She was fair, she said things to your face, without adopting that horrible voice that humiliates you and makes you doubt in front of everybody else, as had happened to me so often.

'It wasn't my intention to upset her.'

'Well, you did, she's very hurt.'

'She could at least realize I don't normally do things like that, you know I never…'

'I know, that's why I need your version of events. I also know it's not enough to be good, you have to look it as well. I think you owe her an explanation, even if you don't give me one. She's just arrived, she doesn't know you… Bear in mind, even though we teachers are older than you, it doesn't mean we're more intelligent or can read people's minds.'

I wasn't able to open up my shell and tell her everything. I couldn't let on this was just another of the tests I was given by Raúl Pernas and his sidekick, Héctor Solla, if I wanted them to stop calling me 'girlie'.

The music teacher had threatened to take disciplinary action against me on account of my irresponsible behaviour, it was like being told I was off to the gas chamber! I was so afraid. They'd inserted one of El Chivi's early discs and told me to press the play button. To my amazement, I heard the following:

I've shaved my balls down to zero
so you can hear the noise when I bang into your behind…

At precisely that moment, there came a 'You have a really great behind, miss', followed by other rude remarks in even worse taste. I nervously started laughing, like everybody else. The teacher turned to address me:

'You'll remember this, you jerk! I won't let you get away with this, you degenerate!'

The things she said struck me as so humiliating that all my words turned into water I kept on swallowing as if drinking at a fountain. My eyes fell to the floor. She quickly left the classroom, and I felt everybody's gaze turned towards me.

'How can you let her call you a jerk?' interjected Raúl Pernas. 'If she calls me that, I'll tell her, "Listen, miss, burn me just a little bit more and you won't be telling anybody because, because I'll cut you open from top to bottom like a hare. So watch out! And don't think about crushing me any more in front of the others."'

'Jerk is just a kind of meat,' it occurred to me to justify my submissive attitude in this way.

At that moment, I felt like a broken puppet and swore to hate her for blaming me. Raúl Pernas and my own fear put my intelligence to the test and, before the teacher returned to the classroom, I came up with my first charade:

'If I fly off the handle, I'm capable of doing anything. Even yesterday, I grabbed a cat that passed in front of me, held it by the neck and twisted until strangling it, without it scratching me once,' I don't know what psychopathic story I'd got this from.

I thought, if I used the same strategies and let my pseudo-murderous ideas run free, I could perhaps protect myself.

How it rained that afternoon! The windows wept constantly. Curro heard about what had happened and told me he'd often seen her cross Inferniño on her way to República Arxentina Avenue around seven o'clock. That same day, I went to wait for her. If she hadn't turned up, it's possible I'd have forgotten all about it, but I was deeply affected and gathered enough strength to tell her about the bullying I was being subjected to and clear the air.

I sheltered in the entrance to a building while the rain did a drumbeat on the pavement and rehearsed like an actor, mentally going through the words I had to say.

The sky cleared. And eventually she appeared. I jumped out in front of her, like a common mugger. My rehearsal had nothing to do with my reaction in reality. Keeping my hands in the pockets of my anorak so she wouldn't see how nervous I was, I said:

'Hello, I...'

She stayed quiet, and I turned white as a sheet. I immediately started trembling. I don't know how fast my pulse was going, but I reckon I was close to having a heart attack.

'Don't worry, André, I know what really went on in the classroom, so please forget all about what I said.'

'Did the school counsellor talk to you?' I blurted out.

'No,' she smiled, 'it was someone else who was present when they changed the CD, someone who clearly appreciates you, but I'm not going to tell you who it was, a promise...'

'Thanks,' I replied and flew away like a dove that's been liberated.

Dove...

How long until our meeting? I feel under pressure, I'm ashamed of all the things she knows about me. It's like I made a film in the nude and now I suddenly had to show my face in front of the audience. I'm trapped inside the sincerity between us. What will she really be like? Not even a photo...

I can always not go. What should I do?

It's all too much...

10

There was far too much that didn't go well for me during the first year of secondary. I couldn't even take refuge in the toilets. The toilets had been taken over by some clandestine bullies.

'What are you doing here?' they asked me, blocking the door while a cloud of smoke slipped out through the crack.

'I have to come in.'

'Outside, go and pee in the corridor!'

They laughed and, feeling submissive, I laughed as well and ran away without daring to tell on them.

That day, I couldn't put up with the wait. I spent the whole break leaning against a wall, squeezing my thighs. I was convinced, if I took a single step forwards, I'd burst. I looked in the direction of the stairs and saw a girl signalling to me; she was from my class, but I didn't know her name. Halima was trying to tell me to use the toilets next to the landing on the stairs. My need was so great I had to climb the stairs slowly, as if holding a glass of corrosive liquid in my hand which was on the verge of overflowing. When I came out of the girls' toilets, misfortune dictated that I should bump straight into Héctor Solla. He told the rest of the school, and that's how I got the nickname 'girlie'.

I learned, if I wanted to use the toilets, I had to pay a tribute: one euro, a good ballpoint pen, my sandwich... I even had to give them my new raincoat on one occasion and then explain at home how it had disappeared as if by magic, but that's another story. To begin with, only people from Raúl Pernas' group were allowed to use the toilets whenever they wanted.

Another, miserable I began to grow inside me; it was time to invent fables, to use the same currency those people used, even if the whole thing was false.

There's always a straw that breaks the camel's back. Mine began to give way when grandpa fell ill. My shell cracked and burst into a thousand pieces. Halima helped me a lot, she didn't run away like the others in my class. That may be what attracts me about her, the fact she didn't change her attitude towards me, despite all the things I said. The trouble is the more I want to be with her, the more I walk away. I feel her proximity like a physical pain, and all because of the credibility given to my macabre inventions: 'I go to the kitchen and grab the sharpest knife I can find…' What utter stupidity!

I carried on deliberately not doing well at school, and one day grandpa came to talk to my mother about it. I don't know what they said, all I know is, as a result of that conversation, I practically moved in with my grandparents.

It coincided with the time grandpa was busy adding wire netting for the birds. Those mazes that were more than a hundred metres in length already occupied half the backyard. He had some huge cages that could be entered standing up and were joined by wide corridors made of wire netting, on the roof as well. My grandfather, who was normally so energetic, seemed to have lost his strength. He kept on clinging to his stomach…

The birds flitted happily from cage to cage while Roque leaped about the yard like a puppy, knocking over everything he came into contact with. Crazy with delight at our presence, the dog kept coming over and then running away… Caco watched him jealously.

'Stay there!'

Grandpa wouldn't let them enter the cages with him. He believed temptations were best avoided and, even though they'd never done anything to hurt a bird, it was clearly not because of a lack of enthusiasm. He put a tape he'd taken from an ancient chest into the old cassette player and turned it on.

'These birds are music lovers, they're crazy about music. See how happy they are! They have no desire to leave, they've turned into comfortable old pensioners, just like me. When the weather's good, we open the cages in case one of them decides it wants to become independent. This time, I want you to let them go. Your grandmother agrees, and you'll tell me how it feels.'

'But there are lots of them!' I tried to calculate. 'How many are there?'

'Exactly a hundred and twenty-one.'

'Do you know them all?'

'And they know me,' he laughed, putting his hand on his stomach. 'As your grandmother says, I was always a bird fancier. Even when I was small, if the parents weren't feeding them or the chicks fell out of their nest, I would take them and raise them myself. And when your great-grandmother was out, hoeing the potatoes, she'd give them any bugs she found, and they'd follow her like little children.'

'Garuda, the finch from the cemetery, was just like a person.'

'I kept a similar bird in my backpack when I was at sea.'

'And didn't they make fun of you for being soft?'

'Soft? I'd be soft if I didn't dare to because of what they might think, don't you reckon? It needed me, and so I took it. Besides, Andreíño, what opinion do you have of sailors?'

'It's just I could never take it to class.'

'Maybe... I think, if I had to look after it, I'd take it with me,' I still couldn't imagine what it would be like to do this in class, and he carried on with the litany of his birds, 'What do I know! See? Those yellow ones there are the famous golden orioles from the fig trees.'

'Do you rescue all of them when they fall out of their nests?'

'No! If I happen to be passing by Teodoro's and think one of them wants to come, I buy it and bring it home. Hey, little fellow, how's it going today?' he talked to the birds and to me at once, which made me laugh. 'There were some people who came, it must have been about ten o'clock in the evening, they had a large box with them. "Here you go!" It was the chick of a big bird. They'd been felling pine trees, found it and, knowing me as they did... We put the box next to the iron stove and went to bed. Around eight in the morning, your great-grandmother could be heard running around the henhouse like crazy. "We have to put the hens away, the sparrowhawk's coming." Two fat birds were circling above the roof and wouldn't leave, they just wouldn't leave... They were the parents and were desperate to get their chick back. I let it go, and they flew away together.'

'Birds are better than people,' I blurted out.

'There are all sorts.'

'Look at my father.'

'There are lazy birds who abandon their children as well, and females who have to raise their chicks without help while the men go off with other females. There are loyal ones too. Lovebirds are loyal, in fact they're said to be inseparable. Then there are those who put their eggs in another's nest, like the cuckoo. Your father's a bit like that, he doesn't know how to build his own nest.'

'He's not like the cuckoo. You told me, if the cuckoo finds other eggs in the nest, it chucks them out to make room for its own.'

'What do you want him to do? Throw Nuria out on to the street? Your father's problem is he forgets, for a nest to be solid, it has to be made with love. He's more like the kestrel. He's only capable of being loyal to his territory, and then he's like those that hover in the air without taking decisions,' he fell silent while tying some cabbage leaves to the roof of the cage. He got down off the stool and made the following suggestion, 'One day, we'll go to Portugal to get a goldfinch. One of mine died, and its partner is very down in the dumps.'

'Is that why you gave it a mirror, to deceive it?'

'Yes, but it's not stupid. When they moult, around the end of summer and especially now, when the cold comes, it's a bad time. Some females get their food stuck in their throats, others die of a heart attack… They take to their nests, they put on a scarf, as I say, and that's the end of that, they don't even complain,' he again grabbed hold of his stomach. 'I'm not having shellfish at a wedding again. They serve up crabs that are far too cold, straight out of the freezer… Oh well, let's leave this. After lunch, I'm going to take you to Teodoro's in Padrón, and you're going to choose the bird you want to save. You'll look after it. And, if you want to devote yourself to breeding birds, be careful who you hook up with. Another woman would not have put up with what your grandmother put up with. Haven't you seen the photos from Extremadura?' I shook my head, and he went into the house.

'Haven't you finished yet, you bird fanciers?' my grandmother came out. 'What happened in Extremadura is unbelievable, but if I didn't leave him then, now it's…' she smiled. 'We'd just got married and were just about to go out when he said, "Wait, I have to give the finch its food," and we missed the cinema because we were too late.'

My grandfather came back with the album, and grandma adopted the role of guide.

'See?' They were on the terrace of a bar, when my father was little. A canary was drinking from the lid of a bottle of water on the table. A man was watching them in amazement. In another photo, the bird appeared on the shower rail of a hotel. 'On that journey, the canary came with us. Oh my! It almost caused an accident. We were on the way to Valladolid, it jumped off the headrest into the back. The car behind, even though it was a better model, wouldn't overtake, it just wouldn't overtake, until we heard this terrible braking sound. They'd been watching the bird jump about and almost crashed into the back of us.'

'We even took it out so it could bathe in the public fountains,' grandpa laughed. 'In Don Benito, we were the star attraction. Boys and girls came running over, "A pet bird, a pet bird!" They couldn't believe it.'

'At night, it would come into the hotel with us and, during the day, stay in the car, in the shade, with the windows a fraction open. After that, there was a lot of mess that needed cleaning up! Come on, you two, off you go!' grandma suddenly shouted while adjusting her watch-strap. 'If you're going to Padrón, you'd better go now, the days are growing shorter.'

On the way there, we carried on talking about the same. My window was a little open, and the fresh breeze carried memories of autumn. Grandpa was especially talkative and turned the anecdote about the canary into an adventure story:

'In the hotel, they must have been thinking, "How can the bathroom be so full of bird droppings?" At breakfast, we'd ask for salad, chickpeas, boiled egg…'

'They must have thought you were aliens.'

'They did look at us a bit strange. In Trujillo, we thought it had got away. We'd already travelled ten miles when it appeared from under the seat like a ghost,' he paused for a long time while a truck overtook us on the road to Caldas, then continued, 'One day, my father-in-law came to our house and wanted to catch it. "Come here now, come here!" He spoke to it too roughly, it grew afraid and flew away. It never came back. It must have been eaten by a magpie.'

Grandpa drove as if a flock of sheep were blocking the road. It took us almost an hour to reach Teodoro's shop next to the station.

We went inside the shop. They had everything. There were even tortoises and raccoons.

'See? When it's time for breeding, we buy the laziest ones a nest.'

'Don't they make their own?'

'Some do, which is why we leave them some dried grass and goat hair.'

'Goat hair?'

'Have a look at this,' he showed me a kind of white, knotted wool. 'The canaries love this best. And those from outside will even use what the others throw away.' He talked to himself, 'Poor immigrants!'

When, some time later, I read that story about the dinghy in class, I understood the true meaning of his lament.

How well Dove writes!

Her voice sometimes fills my dreams…

11

The birds' voices filled the whole shop. We walked around the cages without making up our minds.

'Do you remember the parrot?'

'Captain Flint?'

'That's right, the one that ran loose like the hens. Let's see if we can find something similar for your grandmother, one that pulls on the threads of her knitting like the other. She's been a bit strange recently…'

A parrot appeared motionless, with a sad-looking expression.

'What if we adopted it?' I suggested.

'Do you think it can learn how to knit?'

'She'll teach it.'

We bought the bird. When we put it in the cage, I wanted to caress it, but it started banging on the bars. I didn't try my luck again. We left it on the back seat and undertook the return journey. The radio filled the long silences along the way. From time to time, grandpa would take his hand off the steering wheel and clutch his stomach.

'That wedding… you can't trust anything. You just don't know what you're being given.'

We arrived. Grandma was waiting by the door.

'I was worried.'

'Come on now!' grandpa protested. 'Teodoro's isn't

next door, but it was worth the effort, look what we've brought you.'

I fetched the cage from the car. I again tried to caress it, but the parrot rejected me a second time. I didn't insist because I didn't want to stress it. As the days went by, it calmed down a little, but still wouldn't let me pick it up. It didn't even want me to touch its feet. If it landed on my hand, I had to stay stock-still. It would climb up my jacket and peck at my hair, but still not let me touch it. To win it over, I gave it some chocolate. After a few days, I took it out into the backyard, and the little rascal escaped. It turned out to be an anti-social bird. That's why they'd kept it in a cage on its own.

The parrot went away and, like a bad omen, grandpa also began to leave. He ate very little and kept on weighing himself, as if he'd contracted Davinia's obsession with the scales.

'I stuff myself… and keep on losing weight.'

Nobody could persuade him to visit the doctor, but he did hand over to me responsibility for the birds. And so it was, almost without realizing, I became ever more affectionate towards all that fauna with feathers.

Grandpa changed his habits, he was capable of spending the whole afternoon lying in the sitting room, staring into space. His silences became natural, natural… as water from the mains.

'Did you hear? I'm going to pass them all, like I used to,' I promised.

'In which case, ask for whatever you want.'

'You mean whatever I want?'

'That's right…'

I said it in a quick, distrustful tone, but I said it:

'I want a connection to the Internet.'

'But don't you already have a computer?'

'I share it with Davinia, but that's something else. Internet is used to search for information about a project without having to go to the library.'

'What do you need to know? Something about birds?'

'For example.'

'I can tell you things about birds that don't appear in books.'

'OK, grandpa, but there are other kinds of information.'

'About what? Crickets? I can tell you quite a lot about crickets as well…'

I tried to convince him:

'Other things… It's used to send letters that arrive straight away and it's cheaper than the phone. If, for example, you put the accounts from the bar, you won't need any more paperwork, it'll all be stored there for ever.'

'Is it expensive, this Internet thing?'

'No way! Everybody in class has it,' I exaggerated. 'All you have to do is call the telephone company for free and subscribe. If we buy a computer for here, it'll come with a browser already installed. They give you a device you connect to the computer, a CD with configuration files, and you pay with the phone bill.'

I even persuaded him to get ADSL.

Grandpa left me to arrange it, and I felt like the luckiest person in the world. I couldn't sleep that night. I got *PC World*, *PC Actual*… they had a bunch of useless programs. With these magazines and Curro's help – he was a bit of an expert – we'd soon have everything up and running.

'I have Internet for free!' he said to me once. 'I had to get a wireless card, which I connected to the USB and configured... See? That's the advantage of living in a flat with walls like cardboard. The neighbour has Internet, and so do I.'

In the next-door flat, they had a wireless connection to the Internet. Curro, as soon as he inserted the installation CD, found out about the neighbour's connection. He was razor-sharp! He could send messages via the local network. Ping! 'There has been an error!! Warning from your telephone company: we are resetting the ADSL connection. There will be no connection for six hours. Anything you write from now on could cause you to lose your data. You should turn off the computer at once.' Other times, he'd write 'Important! The virus KZ4 has infected all the ADSL servers of Telefónica in Spain. If you do not turn off your computer at once, you will lose all your data. We hope to have resolved the problem by 23:00 hours.' And he had all the broadband for himself. Other times, he'd use one of his programs and configure his computer to give himself 70% of the connection. The neighbour would be cursing the fact everything was so slow, but not suspect a thing. 'You can only do that to somebody who has no idea,' he'd tell me.

The day I took the computer to my grandparents' house and we installed everything, I didn't move from in front of the screen. Curro came to help me configure it. Grandpa wandered over, and I deliberately tried to get him involved.

'We're connecting at the moment. We're installing a chat program, right?'

'What are you asking me for, Andreíño? I'm too late for all of this.'

'No, you're not, grandpa, it's really easy, you'll see. You install the program, put it on your desktop, a new icon appears…'

'The best thing is to search for an IRC program, you can get into a whole load of channels. Here's the IRcap. The first time the program opens,' Curro was helping me, 'it asks which server you want to connect to, there are hundreds. Choose one from IRC-Hispano, they speak Spanish…'

'You also need an email account,' we typed and talked at the same time, 'you can get one for free. You just go into Hotmail, and that's it. And you can use it for Messenger.'

'If it hasn't already been taken. In which case, you'd have to change it.'

'But it's free! See? Mine is An_sanlo15@hotmail.com.'

'Oh, I see, hot mail…'

Poor grandpa, after the bombardment of well-intentioned first lessons, I even got him to have a go:

'Take the mouse and click twice on one of the icons.'

'Hey, what did you do? You used the left click.'

'No, this isn't for me,' he said through gritted teeth, 'the only mouse I know about is the one gnawing away at my insides.'

I was ecstatic.

'This is the future, grandpa! There are already loads of people who buy on the Internet, who work without leaving the house, who even give lectures… Soon, you'll need it for everything. You won't do anything with your hands any more.'

'Right… That's why, despite all this technology, the mess from the *Prestige* oil spill would still be on all the beaches, were it not for the hands that removed it.'

Grandpa vanished, and Curro and I carried on dreaming…

'Let's create a channel. If we need to, we'll advertise it on the doors of the school toilets, in bars and so on.'

'OK, and let's put "Against the Wind" as our welcoming message,' I suggested, 'that's how seagulls land on the sand.'

'Great,' he agreed.

12

'This is great! Look at this page, it has everything, check it out, it has some unbelievable stories.'

We'd been doing the same all morning. Curro typed in the address www.GenteLive.com, and the following text appeared:

I'm almost eighteen and have spent all my life in a hostel. I don't know anything about my parents, nor do I care. What I mean is I don't want to bore you with my life XD.

My problem is I don't know if I'll be able to look after myself. I have some friends who, when they got to this moment, did all right, but I... I'm afraid because they also told me about somebody who ended up becoming a prostitute. If any of you were in my situation, what would you do? Should I start looking for a job? I need your advice ^_^

PS Thanks to those who help me; to those who plan to embitter my day by talking nonsense, they should know I've suffered so much it doesn't bother me. Kisses to all:D

'This one's like Garuda, her parents abandoned her in the nest, and others had to take care of her.'

'And what are you and I, André? Two finches... Look at

this! Piercings, tattoos, compliments, poems, love letters, votes, photos, those who've registered in the last month... This is amazing! Eighteen thousand girls aged between fifteen and twenty... I click on Valencia, and this one here will send us a topless photo if we vote for her and write her a message. Wow! We could send one from GenteLive. If she answers, that'd be it.'

'Not now, let's chat instead. I registered my nickname yesterday. I called myself "Cut Throat". Pretty cool, huh?'

I already had this leather necklace around my neck, so 'Cut Throat' in memory of my finch was not a bad idea. Mother calls me 'Garuda' whenever she's feeling happy.

'Let's see... Hit IRcap,' Curro had finally given me his place. 'Go in there, in there! #As+plus17.'

'I know... Hey, what's going on here?'

'You forgot to put in your password, and it's disconnected.'

'There you go...'

\<Cut Throat\> hellooooooooooooooooo!!

'Come out, there's nobody there. Try in this one.'
'#Girlfriends?'
'Yeah, yeah, that one.'

*** «Cut Throat ENTERS #Girlfriends»
\<Cut Throat\> anybody thereeeeeeeeeeeeeeeeee!
\<Boootiful16\> dieeeeeeeeeeeee
\<Cut Throat\> whaaat?
\<Boootiful16\> «howdie» new partner :P
\<Leo17_\> nothA I W no idea

<Cut Throat> YRU stickn yr tung ot? :-)
<Boootiful16> :O ur nt so nu thN :((((
<Cut Throat> f i wrt w/o abbrs itz coz I12
<Boootiful16> ok
<Boootiful16> what's your real name? :))
<Cut Throat> where are you from? how many are you?

The messages started getting mixed up.

*** «^Ernes_15^ ENTERS #Girlfriends»
<Cut Throat> my name's Wildemore
<Boootiful16> from Coruña two of us
<Boootiful16> :))))))
<Cut Throat> y :-) ?
<Boootiful16> guess, wild + more :PPP
<Cut Throat> I said «wilde»
<^Ernes_15^> xD xD xD
<[[Xisna]]> XD
<Leo17_> XDDDDD
<Boootiful16> u alone?
<Cut Throat> two of us
<Cut Throat> we should talk about other stuff, no?
<Boootiful16> 2 cut throats?
<Boootiful16> where u from?
<Cut Throat> Coruña as well
<Cut Throat> we should meet
<Boootiful16> which part?

'She's a little annoyed. Tell her... we're from Riazor, I don't know anywhere else.'

```
<Cut Throat> by the stadium
<Boootiful16> Riazor? :OOO
*** «Leo17_ EXITS #Girlfriends»
<Cut Throat> yeah, of course!!!
<Boootiful16> so r we
```

'Shall we change the subject, this is getting a bit boring.'
'Just go straight to the point,' suggested Curro.

```
<Cut Throat> we should meet
<Boootiful16> what 4?
```

'Give it to me for a moment,' insisted Curro.

```
<Cut Throat> for sex :@~~~
<Cut Throat> eeeeeeeeeeeeeehhhhh!!!
<XoUbA_16> «Not here: At the gym, leave a message
for when I get back»
<Cut Throat> just a joke, did we frighten u?
```

'You were a bit brutal.'
'Anyway, from Marín to Coruña…'
'Yeah, you're right. Let's find another.'
'Let's see if the next one has more of a fighting spirit. How about this one? I like the name.'

```
<Cut Throat> I need a psychiatrist unless I can find myself
a girlfriend
```

Curro and I always had fun together. That day, we laughed our heads off.

<Cut Throat> heeeeeeeeeeeeeeeeeeeeeeeeeeelllllppp!!!
<green_cloud> w^ mn?
<Cut Throat> how DY knw im a mn?
<green_cloud> cut throats a mn innit? :P
<Cut Throat> sure itz clevA cloud :-)
<green_cloud> watz it?
<Cut Throat> I want to die :'-(
<green_cloud> y?
<Cut Throat> my girlfriend left me
<Cut Throat> n im despo :'''-(
<green_cloud> :(((((
<green_cloud> DY av a foto on GenteLive.com?
<Cut Throat> nt yet bt im a handsome guy
<green_cloud> DY uz msngr?
<Cut Throat> y?
<green_cloud> so i cn put u on my list of cntcts

'Let's use the fact she wants to go.'
'But do it slowly so she doesn't hang up.'

<Cut Throat> tnx btfil
<green_cloud> :DDD
<Cut Throat> wotU lk?
<green_cloud> Ive 2 arms
<Cut Throat> a bit dum no?
<green_cloud> itz jst I Ily av I leg
<green_cloud> a car axidnt
<Cut Throat> no jk

<green_cloud> im nt joking
<Cut Throat> im sry
<green_cloud> dnt wori
<green_cloud> dats y I dnt av a boyfriend
<green_cloud> n0I wnts 2 X a lame gal
<Cut Throat> dats nt tru
<green_cloud> im tlkN bout }xx of lov
<Cut Throat> :-@~~~
<green_cloud> DY wnt sx W me? :(((
<Cut Throat> yesss :-@@@~~~
<green_cloud> n pRsN?
<Cut Throat> u bet!
<green_cloud> whr DY liv?

'Oh, do you think she lives nearby?' I started getting nervous.

Curro's smile calmed me down.

<Cut Throat> n Andalusia
<green_cloud> yeah n im n Jerez de la Frontera
<green_cloud> u dnt wnt NEfin 2 do W me!
<Cut Throat> itz jst dat i avent got ovr my girlfriend
<green_cloud> @ least tel me wotU uzd 2 do +I cn imajn...
<Cut Throat> wadya wn2 heA?
<green_cloud> DdU tuch her tits?
<green_cloud> myn r amazn

'It's a guy, it's a guy!'
'I can't believe it.'

```
<green_cloud> u der??????
<green_cloud> eh!!! av u gon??????
<green_cloud> ans or IL giv u a virus
<Cut Throat> tak it ^ d bum u :@)
```

'If it was my channel, I'd kick him out.'

'Get out of there quickly!'

Curro left, he was going to go to Carrión, without even suspecting our relationship would start to cool from that moment.

I was dizzy from jumping from one channel to another when I decided to click on where it said 'Dove'. I dared to enter a private chat room:

```
<Cut Throat> wdya lk bout guys?
[Dove] that they listen, that they know how to look with
a glow-worm's eyes...
<Cut Throat> yuk!
[Dove] full of light
<Cut Throat> dats OK thN
```

This one didn't hold back, and I was more careful.

```
<Cut Throat> DY av friends?
[Dove] few
[Dove] it's a question of destiny, chance... like with you
```

I carried on chatting until she left. This is how my cybernetic meetings with Dove began. I spoke to her more in four days than with any classmate in my whole life. I never thought I'd be expecting to meet her today in person or about to run off before it happened. I find it so difficult to trust people! She never wanted to tell me her real name, why does she want to see me?

This meeting worries me almost as much as when I met the Swiss girl…

13

When I met the Swiss girl…

I was in year nine, and my hormones had rebelled against me. I was levitating under the effects of a strange anaesthetic when a burst of applause wrapped in a voice of authority forced me to open my eyes. We were surrounded by half the school. The teacher on duty had just come in, having been warned by some snitch from year eight.

'What's this? Do you think it's right what you're doing?'

My blood rushed into my cheeks. I didn't reply. It was her, Beda, who answered for both of us:

'What's wrong? We were just kissing.'

'And you think that's normal?'

'Isn't it natural? We weren't killing anybody.'

'It's also natural to defecate, but you don't do it in front of everybody else.'

'This doesn't smell.'

'We'll see if your parents think the same.'

'You can tell whoever you like, my mother lets me do whatever I want.'

Beda stood up to the technology teacher while I, having turned into a burning ember, remained rooted to the spot like a pine tree in front of a fire. She'd come from Switzerland and, even though she was only in year eight, she had turned everybody's head; I, in particular, wouldn't even dare look at her. She went around with Raúl Pernas' group, they were like a magnet and always attracted the most beautiful girls. Beda never held back and talked openly about how repressed the girls here were, I... I just limited myself to listening surreptitiously.

'It's different over there. You're just a bunch of innocent finches.'

I was jealous I hadn't been to the same school as her. Most of the girls copied her in the way they dressed, in their blue eyelashes...

That morning, Beda made sure she bumped into me as we were climbing the stairs and addressed me with her admirable courage.

'Where do you go in break?'

Her smile sent a shiver all the way down to my toes.

'I don't know...' I gulped.

'I'll wait for you in my classroom,' she was sure I wouldn't refuse.

I didn't. Even the coolest guy in the school would not refuse Beda. If I managed to go out with her, the mockery would cease. It would be the perfect antidote. What an idiot!

The bell rang, and I hung around until I was the last one there. Nobody was surprised, I used to do that often. With the same stealth I would use to capture a baby red-headed finch from the bushes, I slowly entered the year-eight classroom. I was finding it difficult to breathe. Beda was standing by the whiteboard.

'Hello,' I went over.

I didn't say anything else. Her arms gripped me like a crab's pincers. Even my glasses were sweating. The whole of me turned into a vanilla ice cream at the door of a fiery oven. My hearing and sight melted away. I didn't notice the group of children come in or see anything. I was totally taken up with that kiss that turned to torture as soon as I heard the voice of the technology teacher, who, before leaving, turned to address me:

'You dead fly! Your hair's going to fall out, corrupter of minors!'

But she was the same age as me, what were they going to do?

My mother was busy taking grandpa to the doctors. That saved me. They called and found nobody at home. The incident was forgotten and, on the way out, Beda said, 'See you tomorrow, André.'

The first thing I did when I got home was look at myself in the mirror. I could even see the halo surrounding my head! I went into a mystical state that didn't allow me to concentrate on my schoolwork. I engraved her name in my maths notebook, on the desk, the chair, anywhere I happened to be. I even gave up chatting completely.

The following morning, I could see in the looks of my classmates the admiration and envy they felt, in particular Raúl Pernas: the leader of the class, and I had dethroned him! It was a giddy transformation. At break, Beda sought me out, and we kissed in the corridors, the playground... She didn't mind at all the fact that everybody was talking about us, and I felt like a hero. How little that fable lasted!

I found a note written in capital letters in my pencil case. I thought it must be from Beda and opened it quickly:

BEDA IS WITH YOU BECAUSE
OF A BET.
ALL YOU HAVE TO DO IS
GO DoWn TO THE QUAY
AROUND SIX O'CLOCK
AND SEE WHO SHE'S
REALLY WITH.

My first reaction was to withdraw into my shell, but at around ten to six I was standing by the stone sculpture on the quay. It was the most discreet place I could find. I waited for what seemed like a reasonable time; people passed by, totally oblivious to my concern. It was a little chilly, the wind played at combing pleasure boats while the sea shyly frothed up foam. There was nothing to indicate what the anonymous author of that message had told me. I wondered whether somebody wasn't pulling my leg out of envy for my success with Beda, and I hated them for it.

On precisely that day, the Galician teacher had decided to discuss the Middle Ages, medieval songs and dying of love… I was dying of love for Beda. What an idiot! I was thinking of sending her one of those poems. Fortunately, they were difficult to understand, and I decided against it.

At home, I carried on thinking about the same. I went on Google and started searching… Soon, ping! The little window for receiving messages from IRcap, which I always keep open, informed me that Dove had just gone online. It occurred to me to ask her how good she was at poetry.

[Dove] I even like writing poems
<Cut Throat> would you write me a love poem? :O
<Cut Throat> I need it urgently, it's for a girl
[Dove] can't you write one yourself?
<Cut Throat> me? No, I'm finding it difficult to concentrate. Will you?
[Dove] OK, I'll be like Belisa. She also collected loose words in order to do business with them
<Cut Throat> I don't know what you mean, will I have to pay you?
[Dove] :-) Belisa Crepusculario is a character from Isabel Allende's The Stories of Eva Luna
<Cut Throat> oh, right… will you do it?
[Dove] if it comes to me, I'll leave it in your mailbox

The loud noise of the dishwasher reached me from the kitchen. I said goodbye to Dove and went downstairs. Grandma was tidying up with Luísa and Mario, who had worked in the bar for years.

I noticed something wasn't right.

'Don't worry, Neves, it'll all work out. They did the same to my father, and it was just a case of indigestion,' said Luísa.

'Even if it's an ulcer, with the advances nowadays…' Mario tried to sound encouraging.

Grandma's look was one large tear. I just asked:

'Where's grandpa?'

'Oh, he's in Montecelo Hospital with your mother,' she replied, blowing her nose. 'Apparently, they're going to do some tests…'

'What's wrong with him?'

'I don't know, darling, I don't know. They can't find out what the matter is with his stomach. Ever since that wedding…' she blew her nose again.

My grandfather was strong, and at that point in time my main concern was to preserve my conquest and, with it, the chance to stop being the butt of people's jokes. A poem was a good hook to make Beda fall in love with me. I put a piece of pie and two tomatoes on a plate and sat down at one of the tables. Shortly after that, I disappeared upstairs. I went crazy keeping an eye on the screen, but Dove was nowhere to be seen. I tried writing a poem myself, but it was nothing like the ones that talked of dying of love. Perhaps I wasn't in a hurry to die – even of that. I waited and waited…

My own anxiety sent me to sleep…

14

My own anxiety woke me early the next morning and, before going to school, I saw I had a new message:

From: Dove
To: Cut Throat
Subject: Poem
Here's the file you asked me for. What I did was retouch a poem I wrote before, but don't worry, I haven't shown it to anybody, it's unpublished.
I hope you like it.
Dove

I clicked on the attachment.

FISHING FOR DREAMS

I walk in the port at dusk.
The waves whisper silences wrapped in feathers.
They embrace colours, gardens, whistles…
The bells of your laughter resound in the distance,
words of love that take my breath away.
I suffer from your absence.
Indifference?
I am hurt by what your eyes see…
so near the sun, so blind…

but hope doesn't falter.
One day,
the glow-worms will weave your and my initials
in the valley of night.
I LOVE YOU
You and me,
seated at sunset,
stripped of pretence,
drinking time,
reflected in the glass of the sea,
rocking the hours in that scent…
A kiss filling my mouth with salt,
like this, waiting for dawn,
glinting in the eyes,
like this… holding hands
in the poster for a beautiful love movie.
Swifts sleeping in the air,
birds of the night,
white hearts reflected in a face.
You and me in the same kingdom,
inspecting caves…
Breathing you,
breathing me.
Two insignificant castaways
sunk in the immensity of the sea…
Me, flower, you, little prince:
together gathering sunsets,
beats, melancholies…
seizing the perfume of the ephemeral,
a melody that surrounds us
with blackbirds, sparrows,

doves and cut throats.
Two lovers,
anonymous and free,
shaking in sheets of silk.
Together, fishing for dreams.

It was too long, and I decided to print only from the first 'You and me'. I took out the part that began 'Me, flower…', it struck me as inadequate; besides, it would have been the other way around. I left in the part about birds.

With the poem well hidden in the inside pocket of my anorak, I quickly headed to school. I wanted to give it to Beda on the way in. I sat on the stone wall and ignored the cold by watching people. A couple kissed in the distance. She was suffocating in his arms. I smiled. What incredible smooching! He was like a hummingbird, sucking her lips like they were nectar.

A moment, a single moment later, I understood that the only one with his head in the clouds was me: some live embers hit me in the face, and I felt a searing pain. It was Beda and Raúl Pernas! In defeat, I would have liked to throw myself on my dagger, as Basilio did in the book *Don Quixote* when Quiteria marries Camacho, except mine would have been for real. I hid like a common thief.

I reread the note:

… BECAUSE OF A BET.

Who had written it?
They'd been making fun of me all the time. When I entered

the classroom, I felt so embarrassed! Those looks were needles that stuck all over my body. I grabbed hold of my red leather necklace and tightened it until it hurt. I wanted to roar out, to turn into an elephant and shout so loudly I tossed them through the air, but all I could do was pretend to concentrate on a maths exercise.

'Is this yours? It was on the floor,' I heard the voice of a girl, who placed a set square on the desk.

'Ah, yes,' I said, meeting her open eyes. 'Thanks.'

I found it strange she should talk to me. Halima wasn't exactly famous for being chatty. This was her second year in the school, she'd hardly spoken in the first one, though in French she showed she knew more than anyone. She arrived halfway through the school year and always spent the break on her own. Not all our classes were the same, she went to the language workshop. Now we're together in 9B, and it's going all right. Especially for her, she's even won the odd literary prize.

That day, all I could think about was Beda and the humorous looks of my classmates. My heart was poisoned, my body kept shaking. I'd like to have been braver and said, 'Beda, you're like one of those apples without bugs that gleam in the shop window, you're stuffed full of bad chemistry on the inside.' I was the poet Macías the Beloved the Galician teacher had told us about, this event turned into the worst misfortune of my life... until I got home at lunchtime. Anxiety glistened on Mario and Luísa's foreheads in the form of sweat. As soon as she saw me, Luísa said:

'Your grandma's at the hospital. Take whatever you want from the kitchen and, if you don't have much homework, lend us a hand, Andreíño. It goes without saying there are lots of people today, waiting to be fed.'

I didn't ask, it was obvious something wasn't right with grandpa. That afternoon, putting plates in and out of the dishwasher and seeing to the birds, I kept my soul's concerns at bay. I cleaned the water bowls, took out the leaves and changed the water. I made the birds their purée of seeds and boiled egg, took out the cabbage stalks and replaced them with fresh leaves. They didn't fly away, they were starting to know me. One bird began to eat, and another pecked at it so it would leave.

'That's right, just like you,' I talked to them, 'some of us were born blind and carry on being blind for ever.'

Roque and Caco were outside and limited themselves to listening while wagging their tails. When I came out of the cage, I had three birds on my back. I went back in and shooed them away. I wanted everything to be perfect for when grandpa returned.

The sky, a leaden grey colour, threatened rain.

For the next couple of days, the only faces I saw in *The Birdhouse* were those of Luísa and Mario. I shut myself in my room and racked my brains about the project the technology teacher had given us. I felt a strong desire to keep my promise of passing all my exams and to forget about everything else.

The smell of potato omelette rose from the kitchen, and I went downstairs. I was alone and ate with all the greed of a neglected finch chick. Roque barked, he wanted to come in, but I didn't let him. I threw him a piece of omelette, and he fell quiet. He knew his place.

I even went out on to the street to see if grandma or somebody was coming, but no. On the door was a sign written in large letters:

NO DINNERS UNTIL FURTHER NOTICE

PLEASE FORGIVE ANY INCONVENIENCE THIS MAY CAUSE

THANK YOU

Davinia started sleeping at the restaurant. It was easy to see that grandpa's condition was serious. I didn't ask her. She always said things far too bluntly, and I wasn't in the mood for hearing about more misfortunes.

I went back to my conversations with Dove. I told her I'd been naïve about the poem and hadn't even been able to use it.

[Dove] I'm sorry it didn't work
<Cut Throat> all girls are traitors
[Dove] I'm a girl as well...
<Cut Throat> you're different, it's as if you belonged to me a bit
[Dove] :DDD what an obsession with ownership!
[Dove] isn't it nicer to share?
<Cut Throat> all right, but share... what?

[Dove] dreams, for example

<Cut Throat> nonsense

[Dove] what?

<Cut Throat> rubbish

[Dove] you're in a strange mood

<Cut Throat> it's just that everything has gone badly

[Dove] perhaps you haven't been paying attention to the right person

[Dove] love shouldn't make you spend more time being unhappy than happy

[Dove] don't you agree?

[Dove] hey, are you there???

<Cut Throat> yes…

[Dove] come on then, say something

<Cut Throat> what do you want me to say

[Dove] I don't know… whatever's bothering you

<Cut Throat> I'm worried about my grandpa, men like him should never get ill

<Cut Throat> and I think my father may be involved with drugs

[Dove] what about you?

<Cut Throat> are you my guardian angel?

[Dove] if you let me :DDDD

<Cut Throat> I know full well what can happen, my grandma uses tobacco to kill baby eels

We ended up discussing dogs, birds, music… I told her Kurt Elling had been in Marín:

'It was like flying on the back of a butterfly singing jazz while beating its wings like they were hands…'

15

My grandfather moved his hands like they were wings so I would notice him, but he was at the end of the corridor and I didn't even realize.

When the doors of the lift opened on that fifth floor, my heart was beating as fast as if it had alkaline batteries. I was afraid and didn't really know why. I entered the room and saw an emaciated man with two bottles of saline hanging from a metal frame. A storm was unleashed in my intestines. I went outside. Grandpa carried on waving his hands as I approached. His hair was glistening like a wet pebble. He wasn't the one with the saline!

'How's it going?'

'I'm in charge here.'

He didn't answer my question. He led me through a maze of corridors, showing me how he knew all the patients. His appearance didn't coincide with the tragic atmosphere at home, and this consoled me.

'What, Guillerme, no tests today?' he remarked on passing a man dressed in white. 'Don't forget to take your pills.'

Grandpa took a piece of paper out of his pocket, on which I recognized mother's handwriting.

'You wouldn't believe the restaurant they have here! I'm just glad your mother clarified things for me, I'm feeling a little dazed.' He read aloud, as if preparing for an exam, 'Norvasc, Emeproton, grilled fish here goes by the name of

COD-Efferalgan, with a sachet of Oponaf on the side and, for dessert, Cardyl and a pinch of Orfidal to help with the siesta. All this food, how do they expect me not to swell up like a balloon!'

He put the note away and continued joking with everyone he met, even if he didn't know them.

'You don't look so well today, dear.' He lowered his voice and whispered, 'You have to teach them, see? They think we're all just a number. Come, I want to introduce you to a girl.' I felt cornered, and he realized. 'Calm down, I'm not trying to put you two together. You can't have more than you cope with.' He rubbed his chest with an expression of pain. 'That's right, André, the heart has limited capacity as well. If only we had three, like the octopus…'

We entered room 501. It looked like a gift shop: tiny Christmas trees, plants and figures on the tables, the window sill, the bedhead… everything made using containers for medicines. Sitting in bed, a girl was reading a book.

'Anxo, this is my grandson.'

'Anxos,' she lifted her eyes, 'with an "s", Don Guillerme.'

'That's right, you're not just one angel, you're several.' He turned to me, 'See, this girl is an artist!'

'Pure recycling, just like me! Here you go!' she said.

'No, thanks,' my cheeks went red.

'You can't say no. I have a present for everyone who dares to cross the threshold of that door.'

I took the tiny plant with red petals. I read the words that, in thick black pen, had been inscribed on the tiny white vase:

NEED ONLY BE WATERED WITH A SMILE

and, unconsciously, I watered it.

She also started laughing, but her laughter made me sad.

'How's it going?' I insisted when the two of us were alone.

'Not bad, not bad. I just wish they could find that mouse once and for all.'

'Mouse?'

'That's right, I can feel it here,' he pointed to his liver. 'It's just like a mouse. If I eat, it starts gnawing at me from the inside. Blasted animal!'

'Does it hurt?'

'Bah! Not to worry, they give you things. Trouble is, I don't know, I have the impression the medicine isn't as effective as it was in the beginning.'

'Then it does hurt, you liar!'

'I get by, I get by… So long as it doesn't get any worse.'

His skin was more yellow than usual, and he had a strange look.

Grandpa offered me as a suitor to every woman in a white coat:

'He's a good boy, eh! Why not start a relationship?' He then changed the subject. 'That's enough talking about me, how's that Internet?'

'OK, I've mastered IRcap and Messenger.'

'You what?'

'Programs for talking to people online.'

'For chatting, you mean.'

'That's right!'

'How do you do it?'

'It's easy, Messenger comes with Windows, you only have to add your closest contacts. The rest can be installed without problems by following the steps it gives you. It asks you where you want to install it – disk C, for example – which folder... When you connect, you look for the rooms where there are most people. It has a status window, you click on it twice, and it tells you how many people are connected, there can be more than twenty thousand...'

'What! You talk to twenty thousand people at the same time?'

'No! Everybody goes into their own channels and things.'

He was silent for a moment and then spoke, as if to himself:

'It's OK... I suppose it keeps your mind working; my poor little head...'

'It's easy, grandpa! On IRC-Hispano, you enter with the nickname you want to register, they have a bot, you talk to it, and it tells you how to save things. You press help, and it explains all you need to know: it gives you a registration, an email address... You receive a message telling you if the nickname is free. If it is, you get a password you have to...'

'Enough, enough! I see you're quite the expert! When I get home, I'll have to go surfing...'

'You were a sailor, after all!' I played along.

'You know?' He became more mystical. 'I was lucky enough to live my childhood out in the open, among the ruins of old houses, by the sea... Today, we have more, but we're poorer. We use the car so much, we pass everything far too quickly. We seek goals and forget to go for a walk...' He changed his tone, 'What? How's your grandma? Don't get up to any of your tricks, right? Don't make her angry.' He laughed again, 'Are you looking after the birds properly? They haven't bred for a couple of years, they're getting old like the population of this country. You know they're your concern now, watch out for those finches.'

'Right,' I showed him I remembered, 'some breed in the nests of others, some abandon their eggs, others accept ones that are not their own… A real mess!' I spoke proudly, 'They know me as well as they know you now.'

'Don't forget about the canaries, you have to be careful and keep on insisting.'

'That's right, the blackbirds are easier, they open their mouths like funnels.'

'They're used to their parents sticking their beaks down their throats without even bothering to open their mouths, the way a dove does.'

Dove…

In the days that followed, everything turned virtual. I only had Dove from the chat room to talk to.

What time is it? How slowly everything passes!

Slowly, slowly… last year went far too slowly. We'd just started the Christmas holidays, and Curro had gone back to his home town, Carrión de los Condes. I always said he should walk the Way of St James, but starting at the end. I sometimes bumped into grandma chewing food at all hours of the day. Her forehead was a map of rivers. My mother practically lived at the hospital, doing her work shift or being with grandpa, they always got on well. My sister came because of grandma, but kept herself to herself. And I… I only had the birds to converse with.

My father finally turned up at the house and said hello. I limited myself to giving him a short, piercing look.

'What's the problem? Why didn't you come back to Pontevedra?'

'I didn't feel like it.'

'Well, I miss you…'

'You hypocrite!'

I saw he was about to raise his hand. I stared at him in fury, and it was as if a mechanism stopped him at once. I ran to my room and came back with that stupid box. I opened it in front of him and emptied out kilos of accumulated rage. His eyes popped out of his head.

'Where did you find this? It's not what you think,' he feigned innocence.

I carried on giving vent to my anger:

'You know something? You can't go about pretending to be a fantastic, progressive father when the truth is you never accepted any responsibility. I realize a lot of things I didn't realize before.'

'What things? he wanted me to back up my argument.

'Well, for example the fact that grandpa – your own father! – has been in Montecelo Hospital for three weeks, and it's mother who's with him, while you go about stuffing yourself with this shit!' I was finding it difficult to act the hard man when sparks flew off every sentence that came out of my mouth, but I realized, if you didn't back down, others would think twice before launching an attack. This didn't stop the fire burning in my throat and melting my eyelids. 'You know? You don't fool me any more. You let me down so much that, now I see you like this, I don't even feel sorry for you,' I lied with my words, but not with my tone.

'André, things are not always what they seem, I couldn't take you with me because…'

'What invention are you going to come up with today? Listen, allow me to ignore you, please.' At that moment, the voices of the San Ildefonso children sounded on the radio and, before disappearing behind the door, I shouted, 'With you, we really won the lottery! Just pray nothing happens to grandpa so I don't have to hate you eternally.'

'Wait...'

He said this in a defeated voice that didn't hold me back. I ran and shut myself away in the twelve square metres that had once been his. I would never cry in front of anybody again. I pressed my nose against the window and stayed like this I don't know how long, not doing anything, just waiting for him to knock at the door, to insist, so I could tell him not to come in. But it wasn't necessary. I saw him vanish into the mist. At which point, I ran off up the hill.

I walked a lot that afternoon! There, where the rubbish of the world disappears and only the cries of birds can be heard, I'd been with Curro to discuss our things or be quiet, sometimes we didn't say a word.

I talked as if he was with me. I told him about Dove from the chat room: 'I imagine her white, like her name...' It didn't even occur to me I might one day have the chance to meet her. I talked about Raquel and Nuria, the usurpers, about the change in Davinia, my lack of understanding with my father... It was better like this, with an imaginary Curro I wasn't going to bother with my private demons. They're memories that are engraved, like tattoos, on the epidermis of my soul.

I wanted my father to disappear like he had never existed, to vanish, before suffering what Curro suffered: his father died of a stroke.

16

A stroke...

I was busy in the backyard when some crazy shouting interrupted the evening's calm. Curro appeared outside, subject to a panic attack.

'André, André, my father died! My father died!'

He spoke with a broken voice, he was very frightened. I became frightened as well. I went over to him, and we started walking towards the hill. He didn't stop saying, 'My father died, my father died.' I kept quiet and let him talk. Suddenly, he fell silent. We walked a long way without saying a word. Caco and Roque were with us. Caco, silent as a Christian, clinging to Curro's trouser leg, understood everything and swore eternal love; Roque, oblivious to what was going on, leaped from side to side. We breathed in as deeply as we could and blew out all the air at once, we were pressurized hosepipes trying to wash off abrasive thoughts that scratched like sandpaper.

Little by little, we prised them off walls of silence...

'Whenever I told him off,' I let him talk, 'he would say that sniffing a line of coke was nothing out of this world. He was wrong. A line of coke can kill a man of sixty kilos! He was out of his mind, he would stuff himself with some of that shit and then say, "As in ancient tribes, the situation I'm in today, I have to do this," and I would try to refute him, "Remember the hunter of an Amazonian tribe never took drugs precisely so he wouldn't wound the person next to him with his blowpipe, that would have gone against the survival of his tribe." And he would insist, "But they used to chew coca so they could climb Machu Picchu." I tried to warn him, I always said, "Listen, this doesn't have an antidote, some strokes hide a cardiac arrest on account of coke, it's a vasoconstrictor that causes a spasm in the coronary arteries and leads to a stroke." I know everything about this shit!' Curro talked like this, though I knew all about the beatings his father had given him when he was high; Curro had sometimes run away to our house. And yet he still cried for him! 'Never, you hear,' he stared at me as if guessing my thoughts, 'never did anybody make me feel the emotions he made me feel when he took me down to the sea and talked to me about a Leviathan that on moonlit nights emerged like a marvellous lamp in the exact spot where people shouldn't cast their nets if they wanted to return home. He taught me not to let myself be trapped by the persuasive songs of Nordic sirens. He took me fishing for eels with fishermen from Pontesampaio. At dawn, we'd collect the fyke nets – they weighed a ton! – and carry on working for more than three hours. We once caught the most unbelievable painted eel,' he burst out laughing. 'Once we'd brought the fish back to land, we then had to carry the ten fish traps back to the Arcade Stone. I had such a good time! I haven't seen him for only a day, André, and it feels like a year.'

He burst into tears.

'But, Curro, remember all the stuff he did to you!'

'What do you mean?' he became offended. 'You're not asking me not to love him, are you? Watch out! My father only behaved badly when he wasn't himself. Never – hear me well – never did anybody make me laugh so much about such stupid things. My father was the inventor of laughter, he was capable of turning the fact you'd bitten into a three-tier hamburger without spilling anything into a heroic act. My father was a great guy, André. Who do you think got me into sheltering stray dogs? He did. When he was well, he was the best of the best. He was amazing!'

We sat on a rock and threw pine needles into the distance, although the distance wasn't very far.

It soon started pouring down, but we carried on as before. I don't know why it always rains when someone has died... Both Curro and I liked walking like this, without an umbrella, the water washing us inside. Caco and Roque copied us without protesting. We came out with as much nonsense as we could:

'I hope all coke dealers go up in smoke!'

'I hope they cut off their hands and flay their...'

We said some really stupid things, which may be why we laughed so much.

When we got back to *The Birdhouse*, Curro didn't want to come in, perhaps because there were people in the restaurant, so I persuaded him to come to Pedreiras, since there wouldn't be anybody there. I shut the dogs away and let it be known I was going to Cantodarea, without giving anybody time to notice how wet we were.

We were soaked when we arrived. On the way to the bathroom, like snails, we left a trail of muddy slime. We had a shower and changed into something dry. I lent Curro a sweatshirt and some trousers, and opened the underwear drawer so he could take whatever he needed.

That Saturday, my mother was on night shift, which is why I had initially decided to stay at my grandparents'. Curro still had the colours of anxiety in his eyes, which broke my heart. In those smart trousers, in defeat, he looked a lot smaller.

'It's stopped spitting, do you want to go outside?'

'As of today, nobody's going to ask for me, so we can do whatever you like,' his sorrow kept him in a state of chronic drunkenness.

I felt I had to come up with something that would ease his affliction. His mother, who was also caught up in drugs, had vanished from his life a while back. I decided to grab a bottle of vodka that must have been sitting on the dresser since the beginning of time.

'Come on, today we're going to find out what it's like to get really drunk!'

Curro refused, but the pain of seeing him like this made me persuasive. Nobody would notice the bottle had gone.

We drank until we'd finished it, and our courage automatically grew.

We moved closer together until we were almost embracing and, in an intimacy that stank of vodka, Curro started singing:

'"Get out a paper, I'm preparing a cigarette and a lump for a joint,"' he was unrecognizable. 'Come on, join in! This was the old man's favourite song. '"Keep going, keep going, keep going, keep going... The solution is not in charity, so long as there's misery, there won't be any freedom."' Suddenly he started shouting, '"Welcome to Planet Skuuuuum! You need to be lucky when you are born!"'

We both doubled up laughing and couldn't stop. We were in a bad way.

'Shall we go for a walk?' I said, trying to sound lucid.

'Where are we going like this?'

'To Pontevedra!' I shouted in a captain's voice.

We walked all the way down Cantodarea until we reached the avenue, which we crossed. We were overwhelmed by an unusual sense of happiness. We talked strangely and laughed at everything. I can still hear the cars on the motorway blaring their horns, but we were far too euphoric, our blood pressure and temperature had shot through the roof, to realize the danger we were in. We crossed without looking and reached the wooden footbridge. We carried on walking next to the motorway, alongside the estuary, staggering from railing to railing, from port to starboard. The evening was drawing to a close, and the cars seemed to have secretly agreed all to come from the other direction and dazzle us with their lights.

Curro continued with his performance of songs by the punk band Ska-P, his father's all-time favourite. That night, they turned into our idols as well, and we became solitary freaks obsessed by their songs. I don't know how long we spent on the footbridge, laughing at the cars, at the seagulls playing at jumping over waves, at the birds scratching the only clear patch of sky and turning the night into a postcard, at the sea... I decided to dance and drop my trousers like I was being attacked by ants. I was determined to alleviate his suffering, even if I'd forgotten its cause. I had a pain in my stomach, my temples... everywhere!

We reached the second section of the footbridge to the estuary, and Curro, in a kind of metamorphosis, decided to start running down the iron steps. He ended up rolling down the next flight of steps, which were made of stone. He didn't stop until falling face down in the estuary. It was lucky the tide was out. I ran after him and helped him lift his head out of the mud. I could barely stand up myself. Curro started holding his stomach and moaning. Suddenly, he got up and, clinging to the steel railing, vomited on the stairs. It's amazing what can fit inside a stomach, he was like a pump cleaning out a sewer! All at once, the stench had a domino effect, and I vomited behind him. As our physical malaise went down, so our souls' disquiet increased. The breeze made us feel better, we climbed several steps and sat on the night's railing.

'It stinks!'

'That's not just us,' I pointed out, 'that's the rubbish they dump in the estuary to stop it being so pretty. The cellulose factory is far too near and has a bad smell even if they cover the façade in neon lights. But you just keep on looking at the water coming towards us, right?'

'All I can see is I need to start working.'

The idea of Curro working made us laugh all over again. Our laughter was so loud it scattered the clouds, and the island of Tambo was left without a roof.

'There's the first star.'

'That's Venus, my father told me,' and all his euphoria came tumbling down.

I grabbed him by the shoulder. The noise of the cars on the avenue disturbed the quiet produced by the water. Not far from where Tambo lighthouse converses with the sea, a small boat ignored the path of red signals and followed the green ones. The lights of Lourido, Combarro and Portonovo painted vertical lines in the water. Right there and then, we swore eternal friendship. We started beating rhythms with our feet, with our fingers on our lips, with our teeth, banging our thighs with our hands...

'We could form a duo.'

'That's right, and call it "Two Birds in the Night".'

The shrill cry of an owl came from behind us.

'The world would be better if there were only birds caressing the hours… and crocodile heads,' I added, gazing at the silhouette of the island, which was just like the head of a large black crocodile with its body in the water.

'And dogs…'

We were incapable of keeping up a fluid, coherent conversation. From time to time, my eyelids would close, and I would hear Curro say something, but I couldn't faithfully reproduce what it was. I don't know how much time passed or what we talked about, if we talked about anything.

I felt the bite of a morning of mists, like our spirits, on my back and realized the water, bathed by dawn, had almost reached our feet. The sun, which was about to rise in the east, was already threatening an obstinate moon that challenged it from the estuary. We got up, feeling numb, painful, and dragged our tiredness of body and soul across the wide, wooden corridor. The avenue was dressed for a Sunday morning.

'It's so cold! It's as if the air had stuck its icy teeth in. What the hell were we doing here?' I talked through a mouth that was dry from the lack of saliva.

'You look amazing! You're just like a gatherer of shellfish, all you need now is a bucket and rake.'

'Let's go to my house, it's nearer,' I decided, unsure whether he would understand my snuffling pronunciation.

I didn't want to go to Curro's house, I couldn't sleep where there was a dead man.

We went straight to bed without even taking our shoes

off. I didn't even remove my glasses. We slept until it started getting dark again.

We were woken by the smell of food, which was in sharp contrast to the stench coming off our clothes in the bathroom. My mother had undressed us without our realizing. She already knew about the tragedy.

'Which do you prefer, breakfast or dinner?' We didn't have the energy to reply. We sat at the table in silence. Mother placed a magnificent potato omelette, a bowl of fruit and a jug of chocolate milk on the table and said, 'Eat this. If you want more, look in the fridge, but don't eat the stew for tomorrow, otherwise there won't be time.'

She went over to Curro, gave him a kiss and whispered something in his ear. She came over to me and told me I'd done well not to leave him alone. His father wouldn't be buried until Monday morning because of some rule about twenty-four hours.

Poor Curro! Since he left for Carrión and grandpa got ill, I haven't called him. He hasn't looked for me either... I think he's upset. I used to be something like his pet dog. If he said, 'Be still!' I wouldn't breathe until he said, 'Move!' I trusted him a great deal.

The last thing I heard is that he was hired by the town hall to help set up summer concerts, which allowed him close contact with his father's idols. That was a few days ago. I bumped into him in the supermarket queue. He was wearing a white neck collar and a T-shirt that revealed a recent wound. On his left eyebrow flashed the pyramid-shaped extreme of an earring. We hadn't seen each other for such a long time I wasn't sure how to strike up a conversation, but the fear of him ignoring me made me react.

'How's it going?' I greeted him.

I found him changed, cold. He had a lost look that unsettled me. There was a cathedral of distance between us.

'Well… it's going well. I was employed by the town hall and now I do lots of work for Ska-P. I've travelled to half of Europe. I was in Holland, Switzerland, the UK… We're due to go to Mexico. It pays very well.'

I could sense he was lying. The only part that was true was that Ska-P had given a concert in Marín some time before and, to set up the stage, they'd hired some people. As far as I know, the group no longer goes on tour, but I didn't dare contradict him and went along with what he was saying:

'Where did you get that collar from?'

'There you go, you red and me white. Oh, I fell off a jenny. I was setting up the lights seven metres off the ground, had just got back from an errand and didn't realize one of the spots was on. I touched it, and it gave me a shock. I jumped backwards and fell on my back. It didn't do my vertebrae any good,' he'd always had problems with his spine, 'but I'm OK! On Thursday, they're starting a tour of America, and I'll be with them.'

'But weren't they just a bunch of beer-swilling louts who got up to all sorts of tricks on stage?'

'No way! They're fantastic guys. In fact, I was feeling a little lost and, thanks to them, things got better,' I noticed the sting in his remark. 'The record label just wants them to come across like that, it's a front they put on for the public.' I didn't dare ask him anything else, but he carried on talking, 'So I've just got back from the medical centre in Virxe da Carme, they had to have a look at this tattoo,' he showed me the wound.

'Doesn't it hurt?' was all I could think of saying.

'Of course not!' he replied arrogantly. 'Other things hurt more. If you don't go too near the bone, it doesn't hurt. It's a kind of eel I designed myself that nobody else has. I'm like them, I know I can't grow if I hang around the place where I was born, I have to seek out a life for myself far away. It was oozing ink and got a little infected, but it's OK, the wound has closed and I went to have it touched up. How are things with you?'

'OK… nothing much. I don't know if you heard about my grandfather.'

The promise of eternal friendship, which I hadn't kept, and the sad look that contradicted what he was saying ate away at my insides. I put a hand in my pocket, hiding the unease that tingled in my fingers.

'Yeah, that was later on. I was in Carrión by then, you know.'

'Not to worry! Hey, look!' I took out the note that had been in my pocket for a while. 'It's in Arabic, perhaps you know someone who could translate it for me.'

My intention was to have a reason for meeting again.

He took the piece of paper, and we said goodbye without making any promises. I watched him disappear like a grey bird lost in the mist…

17

Like a grey bird lost in the mist…

Having argued with my father and watched him disappear into the mist, having walked over that wet ground, building myself up again, I sat on the same rock I'd sat on with Curro some time before. I could still feel the heat of his body while a gust of warm wind licked my face. I decided to throw some pine needles, this always relaxes me. Recent memories crowded into my mind: my father was very thin, he must have been under sixty kilos. I got up again. There were two weeks of uninterrupted rain, of clouds discharging electricity and skies roaring like cornered beasts. On the ground, I spotted a couple of dark lumps at the foot of a tree. There had to be a barn owl or a little owl in that oak. I broke the lumps with my heel and discovered some tiny bones that were still fresh, the remains of food the owl had regurgitated. I looked into the hollow of the tree, but couldn't see it.

I returned, accompanied by the ghosts of my memories. My grandparents' house was full at last. I recognized my mother's old Fiat parked in front of the bar. When I went in, Davinia came to meet me.

'Is grandpa here?' I asked.

She looked towards the stairs, and I climbed them three by three. I found grandpa in his room, sitting next to a small folding table, with pillows everywhere. He was sucking on a velvet crab's pincer. Grandma was watching him. There was something in the atmosphere that dampened my euphoria. Damned conjunctivitis! This blasted malady was affecting my whole family.

'Hello, Andreíño,' said grandma without looking away from my grandfather.

'Hello,' I replied.

Grandpa barely raised his head to smile at me and carried on sucking at those pincers grandma squeezed for him and gave to him with the food already showing. He took them with delayed movements, all his energy had gone. I went over, stroked his hair and, without saying anything, he looked at me slowly, very slowly. At that point, I felt a corrosive substance consuming my insides. The whites of his eyes had turned a deep, phosphorescent yellow colour.

'Come on, darling, you only have these ones to go.'

Grandma was referring to some pills on the table. Grandpa pushed them from side to side with one finger, like someone playing noughts and crosses, but didn't put them in his mouth. She took one and gave it to him. She immediately put a glass of water to his lips, and grandpa drank, spilling half the liquid on the napkin hanging from his pyjama collar.

'Look, Guillerme, look who's here. It's Andreíño! Andreíño came to see you, my darling,' grandma spoke in a strange way.

She kept on smiling, but neither her tone nor her gaze corresponded with the euphoria of her actions. She poured some syrup into a spoon and brought it to grandpa's lips, but he raised his hand and pushed it away. The white paste fell on his pyjama trousers.

'Nflcknway!'

He protested in an unfamiliar voice that seemed to come

from far away. He was incapable of pronouncing his words clearly.

'He's not the same, darling, he's just not the same,' grandma apologized.

I ran out of that room with the sensation somebody had torn out my entrails. I entered the living room, not knowing where else to go. In the middle of all the mess on the table, I saw various dishes with ampoules, pills, syrups, syringes… and a piece of paper with a kind of galactic menu. Underneath, the word 'DIAGNOSIS'. I read 'Gastrointestinal stromal tumour POSITIVE'. I jumped when I felt a hand on my shoulder.

'We have to do our best to make grandpa feel comfortable, OK?'

It was my mother.

We stayed for a while with our noses pressed against the window. Two blue plastic bags played at being birds.

I couldn't go back into that room. I watched him from a distance. It made me desperate to see how he struggled to sit up in bed and my mother anxiously tried to prevent him.

'You can't get up, Guillerme! Like this, like this…'

She surrounded him with more pillows, but grandpa slouched like a gooey substance. It occurred to me to take the telephone downstairs and call my uncle and aunt. I wanted them to search out the best doctors in Madrid, since grandpa wasn't well, but Aunt Eulalia's reaction made me hate her for ever:

'André, you're a big boy now, you have to realize things don't always turn out the way we want them to. Grandpa has galloping cancer. There's nothing that can be done that isn't already being done. You have to accept the worst.'

The worst! It could still get worse. Things were changing so quickly!

Never in my life had I been so free, I could do whatever I liked. I scurried off up the hill. There, I started thinking about what Dove from the chat room had told me: 'He might get well. I know of a girl who was like that for days. Her father talked to her all the time, not paying attention to those who said she was clinically dead, and, when everybody had given up hope, she opened her eyes. She got better.'

I went back, determined to vanquish the terror of entering that room. I stopped at the door, I felt my heart beating wildly. I took a deep breath and went in. There, next to grandpa, all my fears vanished. I carefully positioned the cushions between his ankles so he wouldn't get sores, he couldn't move. My mother turned up next to me and threw me out:

'Go on, you, go for a walk.'

I wanted to hate her, but the dejected look in her eyes only made me obey her. I went to the centre and wandered around Jaime Janer, Doutor Touriño and all those streets that still bore the perfume of Christmas carols, lights and people in a hurry. Christmas Day and New Year's Eve had already passed, but in our house we hadn't even noticed. It was a not unfamiliar voice that reminded me of it:

'Happy New Year, André!'

'Oh, hello!'

I hadn't gone far when I heard the voice again:

'Wait a minute, do you have something to do?'

I stopped and shook my head. It was Halima, but I didn't want to talk to anyone. She came over and looked at me.

The blood rushed to my cheeks as if they'd been pinched. The black jet of her eyes unsettled me. She walked beside me for a good while, neither of us saying a word, in polite silence. She stopped in front of a shop window, and I stopped as well.

'Will you come in?'

I followed her into the shop. She wanted me to approve of things with my eyes, but I didn't react. She ended up buying a colourful hat and a matching sky-blue scarf. We queued up to pay and left. Outside, I pretended I was in a hurry, I didn't want to stay by her side. The way grandpa was at the moment, I didn't have the right to feel happy.

'Why don't you buy a bird or two to keep you company? They're very tame,' she held me back.

'I have lots. I have more than a hundred birds. When the weather improves, I let them go,' grandpa was still in my head. 'I have to go, see you.'

'I hope your dreams come true!'

My dreams... I didn't even know whether I had any dreams, I didn't even know what house I was going to sleep in. In the end, I headed back to Pituco. I took the key from under the old azalea pot, the way we'd agreed as a family secret, and went in. Out of inertia, I went straight to the bathroom upstairs. Ever since I was a child, I'd been used to not using the customers' toilets. On the marble side around the bathtub, I saw a large plastic bottle. It was almost full of a dark liquid like Coca-Cola. A few lines indicated the capacity. Next to it was one of those male urinals, also made of plastic, that look more like a duck than a chamber pot. It was grandpa's urine.

Every day, all the time, there appeared new signs that things were getting worse. Everything at home reminded me of it. I got into bed. I didn't feel like talking to Dove, I knew she'd try to console me and I didn't want this. To forget about grandpa's situation seemed to me a betrayal.

What I wanted was to shout until I burst the air's eardrums…

18

The air's eardrums were bursting…

The birds were making a lot of noise that morning. I got up early and looked out of the window, I always do this when I wake up. The sky threatened rain, and the small car for home visits parked next to the fence. Out got a man and a woman with heavy bags, as if they'd just arrived from the supermarket. Almost immediately, the bell rang. I stayed in my room until I saw the car pull away, then I went down for breakfast. I could hear voices in the kitchen, I didn't dare go in, but this didn't stop me hearing:

'I want only the best, and for there to be a choir, I don't care how much it costs. A bus from Bueu and another from Estribela. There are lots of people there who know him and love him well…' Was grandma arranging… a party?

A miracle! Grandpa was getting better. I made a firm resolution never in life to do things he didn't like, to learn how to face up to life… They were organizing a surprise to celebrate his recovery. I could invite Halima, having paid her so little attention the day before, I could call Curro. After the hurricane had passed, I would rebuild my inner city.

'Where do you want it to be?' insisted an unfamiliar voice.

'I'll come with you and show you the place,' said my mother.

I was just about to enter the kitchen, leaping for joy, when…

'You know, the way we were in bed, in the niche on the right. And I want the wreaths…'

It was as if a truck had caught me on a zebra crossing and smashed me to pieces. It wasn't fear, it was… something else. But he was alive! I didn't have the stomach for breakfast and climbed the stairs. I went to grandpa's room, standing by the door for a long time before going in, then walking towards him on tiptoe, I didn't want the floorboards to creak. His eyes were closed, I leaned over him. His breathing was a little agitated, but he was breathing!

'Grandpa, are you asleep?' I went a little closer. I sat on the bed and took his hand between my own. At this point, an eyelid flickered. 'Can you hear me?' He looked like he was about to laugh.

'He can't hear you. They're muscular spasms,' declared my mother from the doorway.

The look I gave her had all the force of a tornado, and she scurried away. Were they losing their minds? Grandpa could hear, the beats in his fingers were different when I talked to him. And I talked. I talked a lot.

'Don't worry, right, champ? You stay calm, you'll get better, you'll see. You know something? The birds are fine, I look after them, but they're always asking after you. Ah, you were right! The weaver's not pink any more, it turned grey. I have the impression this year it's going to breed. As soon as you come, we'll have to start preparing the nests. You remember the goldfinch?' Grandpa's breathing became faster and more laboured. 'Calm down, take it slowly, like this, that's right. You remember it was so dumb it couldn't learn how to move from one cage to another? Well, now it goes around them all and gets it right the first time,' I talked in a happy voice so he wouldn't notice the drone in my soul. 'Yesterday, I rescued a robin,' I lied, 'that was a bright one, in half an hour it had been around all the cages. You're right, grandpa. They're like people. Some of them make do with what they have, others search out a life for themselves, they're brave like you, champ,' I felt him getting ever more distant, grandpa was leaving, and I couldn't stop talking. I had the impression that, if I stopped, he would stop. 'Ah, something I didn't tell you. You remember that crow Mario brought us? It wasn't happy, and I did what you would have done, I left the door open, and the little mite flew away,' this was true. 'I'm like you, I won't keep them back by force. Yes, I know, don't worry, I understand you. Yes, yes, that was the one that used to peck at Luísa's nails whenever they were painted with red varnish. It struck me as so nervous I let it go, I don't know whether it will want to come back. These days, there are crows in the pine trees, they all alight on the highest branches, but there's one that's a lot more confident than the others, it alights further down, I'm sure it recognizes me, it's the same one. When I go out into the yard, they all fly away, but this one moves its head, opens its wings and waits for a while, it's not frightened.' Grandpa's breathing became slower and more erratic, life was beating inside his body like a bird in a sealed glass cage. One moment, it seemed he'd forgotten to breathe, the next he wanted to consume all the oxygen in the room, then he'd succumb to pauses that stuck in my throat while I carried on with my false euphoria. My hand was getting hotter, or his was getting colder, I couldn't be sure. Even so, I didn't stop talking. 'You know? I'm going to teach you how to chat, it's great fun,' I felt him letting go of my hand. I stroked his hair with the other and noticed it had acquired a strange electricity. It stuck to his scalp like a magnet, it wasn't like normal hair. 'You know? I met a girl while chatting who calls herself Dove. You and she are the only ones I share things with. She's very clever. I imagine her like a dove, all dressed in white. I like it when I'm talking to her. You stay calm, champ. I bet you can't guess who's back in my class. That girl from abroad, no, I don't mean the Swiss one! For me, it's as if she's turned into a lizard. No, I mean Halima, you know? I met her in the street, and she asked me to go with her to buy some things, she wanted me to buy a bird, she didn't know we already have all sorts. I'll introduce her to you one day. She might even like me. If only I could be sure… At least I know she likes birds. Ah, you'd better get well soon, without you Roque's been going over the top. He might even be gay, I've seen him clinging to Caco's tail and giving it all he's got, like he wanted to screw him,' I laughed, but the words were burning in my throat. 'You know? They say I'm really lucky to have a grandpa who let me connect to the Internet, and it's true,' my mouth was becoming dry, but I didn't want to stop. I felt as if I was holding on to a slippery bar with both hands and, beneath me, there was a large abyss. I had to carry on. 'Ah, I forgot to tell you! I even passed technology this time around,' I lied, 'all of them, I passed every single exam with excellent marks. And, while you're not well, I've been looking after the birds. Don't you worry about them, they're feeling very well. They've even acquired a taste for Primal Scream. When the plants start seeding, if you haven't fully recovered, I'm going to do what you said: open the doors, give them a return ticket, and they can do whatever they like. Don't you worry about it, everything will be fine. Aren't you lucky to have a grandson who loves you so much, eh? But then, who wouldn't love you? Even the sea protected you when you were on your boat, that one you rebaptized with an androgynous name as soon as I was born, I know why all right, *Nevesandré*, your two great loves, right?' I imagined Raúl Pernas, Héctor Solla or one of their gang could see me, and I didn't care. I felt as if, through his hand, something of grandpa's was coming inside me for ever, like his brain had fused with mine. 'The sea never gave you much trouble. "The sea kisses the feet of women waiting on the beach for boats laden with nostalgia", I haven't forgotten anything you told me. You remember that cloudy day there were hundreds of seagulls on the beach, all of them facing the wind, combing their feathers? "They're pointing to the north," you explained. I remember every minute we've spent together. The two of us were barefoot, walking along the seashore in search of strangely shaped stones, "of the kind the sea likes to spit out from time to time," you told me, and the seagulls took flight and passed just over our heads, "you stay with me and don't be afraid." Remember? On the sand, there were only our footprints and those arabesques left by the seagulls' feet. I still have the stones we collected last time on top of my desk. The ones that were in the water looked prettier, and you said, "See, André, the wet ones are like you, all shining," you took one and let it dry on the palm of your hand, "Now it's just like me, we old people lose our water and don't gleam any more," and I went and threw water at you until you shone like a stone in the sea. I was never afraid while I was with you. Now it's your turn. Don't you be afraid either. Stay calm, breathe slowly, everything's going to be fine,' the air in the room was not enough for him. 'I promise to have a better relationship with my father. In fact, we've already settled our differences,' I lied again. 'Don't you get upset about anything, OK? Don't you suffer, all right?' Grandpa's hand was frozen, and I couldn't continue. I don't know why I did this, but I gave him a kiss and said, 'Grandpa, you always listened to me when I asked you. Please, rest now, stop breathing, leave…' The words stuck in my throat, and grandpa didn't breathe any more. He put on a scarf, became like a bird, and I felt exhausted.

Suddenly, the rain ceased to be a threat, and the sky emptied itself on the windows…

19

The sky emptied itself on the windows…

And cried for me.

And reminded me of that story… A girl was crying because her doll had fallen into a dry well. She cried so much she filled the well and managed to rescue the doll, which was floating on the water. But that's all it was: a story.

The dogs whined while I felt a sudden calm. I knew, when someone was dead, you had to lower their eyelids and, without feeling any horror, I put my hand on his eyes. Someone blew their nose behind me. I looked around. The doctor had invaded my privacy.

'Excuse me, I…' she made an attempt to apologize.

I didn't say anything. I ran out of the room and shut myself inside my fortress. I turned on the computer. I can't remember if I sent a message. After a short while, I heard a variety of voices on the landing…

I don't know how long it was before someone woke me.

'Here you go, it's hot,' my mother had brought me a glass of milk. 'Come on, turn off the computer, you left it on, and start getting ready if you want to go to the funeral home. I'll come and pick you up later, if you have no one to take you. I'm going now,' and she left a set of clothes on my chair.

I went straight to the bathroom. In the room that had been set up for grandpa, the folding bed that had been there for the last few days had gone, it had been turned back into the sitting room it was normally. The medicines had disappeared, it smelled clean. There were just a few unused syringes on the table. Luísa and Mario were ordering everything.

'I shall reincarnate as a bird to come and sing you morning serenades, crowned like a poet with a laurel wreath,' I seemed to hear grandpa saying, and it cracked me up to think of a bird with grandpa's face. I went out into the yard and was overwhelmed by the din: the birds were jumping like crazy, colliding with the wire netting. Some were wounded and had fallen on the ground.

'Mario, quick, come outside! Quick, come here!'

'There must be a mouse or something,' he declared.

We found nothing to explain the reason for such a disturbance. We continued to watch carefully. Roque and Caco were very excited and barked at the sky. A crow cawed, tearing the wind to shreds. A magpie soon appeared, and the birds, in terror, banged into everything.

'That blasted magpie!' Mario understood what was happening.

The magpie wanted to tire them out and, when they couldn't resist any more, it grabbed the ones that had fallen down exhausted in the linking corridors from outside.

'Its nest is up there!' I shouted, pointing at a eucalyptus. 'Can't you see it?'

'No way! It's far too early to breed in January, though the weather recently has been so warm…'

I felt really annoyed. I grabbed a stone and flung it at the murderous bird with all the intensity of my rage, aiming so well that its nest immediately dropped out of the tree. It landed on the laurel that grows by the southern corner of the fence, whose branches absorbed the impact. I went over and couldn't believe my eyes when I saw a chick in the still intact nest. I took it inside, the chick wasn't to blame for its mother's actions. I fetched one of the unused syringes, beat an egg, and filled it with that yellow liquid. It moved so much it wasn't easy to pinpoint its beak, and I didn't insist. I left it in a tall box next to a radiator in the kitchen and went with Mario to the municipal mortuary.

There were lots and lots of open umbrellas clustered in front of the entrance. I used to like the rain, but on that day it bothered me. People stared at me, but, as if grandpa had taken all my prejudices with him, I didn't mind. I entered room number two and found my father surrounded by a great deal of expectation. He pressed his hands against the glass separating him from the coffin and was making a real scene:

'I killed you, father! I killed you because I didn't know how to behave. I promise you I'm going to change. I'll be different, father…'

People muttered disparaging remarks while he carried on spelling out intimacies, and a dagger of rage sank into my chest. My father was always in the habit of making promises that quickly vanished in a puff of smoke. Someone, I think it was Luísa, told me there was no point staying and took me straight to the church.

In front of the church, there must have been more people than at the funeral home. Next to the entrance, I encountered the lopsided smile of Halima in her colourful hat. She was the only classmate I saw there.

Inside, during the funeral, all I know is my mother whispered to me:

'I want you to go to the front and thank people, Andreíño, OK?'

'Thank them for what?'

'For being with us. Grandpa would like that.'

'Does it have to be now?'

'No, right at the end. I'll tell you when. All you have to do is read this.'

My blood pressure increased to levels that were almost impossible to bear. I glanced at the piece of paper:

I would like to thank you in the name of my family and in my own name for being with us at such a difficult time.

I wasn't sure I could do this.

A gentle push, and I was standing in front of the congregation, behind a lectern, with a microphone at my lips. I went into a kind of ecstasy that made me put on a scene like that of my father:

'My mother would like me to thank you... But what I really feel like doing is talking to you about my grandfather Guillerme. I know it might sound stupid: if you're here, it's because you know him, some because you're guests of the restaurant, others because you were with him at sea. Some of you may have known him from when he was like me, or from before, I don't know... But there are probably others who don't know anything about him,' I was getting a little flustered, but I couldn't stop. The words came without my asking. 'I just want you to know my grandfather was a great guy, what I mean is he was fantastic, and I'm not just saying that because of the pocket money he gave me each week, or…' some of those who had gone outside came back in, and I rose to the occasion, like I was high or something, 'and I don't mean because of the courage he showed when the *Nevesandré* was letting in water miles from the coast and, while the other sailors despaired of saving their lives, grandpa started peeling an orange and eating it in front of everyone so they would see how calm he was, how confident of being rescued. And they were rescued. And I don't mean because… I don't know if he's the person who knows most about birds, what I do know is he's the one who loves them best,' and I turned towards the coffin. 'Grandpa, I know you can hear me, you always listen to me. We have another bird. A magpie chick. And I don't mean because of all the times he told me his love story, which he turned into something unique,' I searched for my grandmother, who was sitting next to my father. 'Grandma, I love you loads, but grandpa… grandpa was grandpa. And I don't mean because he looked at me like I was Bill Gates whenever I told him something about the Internet. I mean because…'

I came out with intimacies and didn't care if I was making a fool of myself. The attention people paid me filled me with a strange euphoria. I went so far as to reveal it was me who had been lucky enough to close his eyes and this had given me peace. Suddenly, a bird, probably escaping from the downpour outside, entered the church and started flying all around me. The energy left me, the words turned into saliva and smothered me. I fell silent, but stayed where I was. Everybody started clapping. I glanced back at the coffin and burst into tears.

Outside, the storm abated, and there were kisses and

hugs... like people were congratulating me. It felt so strange! The bird disappeared into the sleepy cotton of the clouds. Suddenly, several flocks of starlings drew figures in the air. They formed and unformed waves at high speed, darting from side to side – in honour of grandpa, I thought.

'I envy you,' whispered Halima.

I felt her hot breath next to my ear, as if I'd gone down to the seashore and was dancing in the foam, but I didn't understand what she meant. At that moment, it was as if she'd spoken to me in Arabic, just as when, after the final exams, the Galician teacher started talking about different languages and dignity, and someone, knowing how easy it was to sidetrack the teacher, suggested Halima practise Arabic in class. The stage was set.

The teacher asked her to come to the whiteboard, whispered something in her ear, and she started writing. He then asked us to guess what it said. Of course, none of us got it right, but we were all amazed by the spectacular form of writing, which looked more like embroidery than a written code. We soon found out these were our names in Arabic and copied our own.

When Halima sat down, she wrote something in my notebook:

الحمامة و المقطوع الرأس

'It's a treasure map,' she said. I tore out the sheet and put it in my pocket. I stared at her like an idiot, imagining it said 'I like you a lot' or something. I gave it to Curro the last time I saw him for him to decipher the message or so I could have an excuse to see him again.

20

I had a special reason to see it again...

I went to the kitchen to check how it was. The bird had lost its eyes! They'd been replaced by a yellow crust. Even so, it was breathing. Mario wasn't there, and I didn't know what to do. When I touched it, it started opening its beak, I thought it was suffocating. That's when I realized the business with the eyes was because of the egg. I put some warm water in a cup with a tiny bit of soap and passed a wet cloth over its eyes. The chick trembled, but let me work. When it opened its eyes, they looked so bad I thought I'd messed them up for ever. At precisely that moment, my father turned up.

'What are you doing?'

'There's something wrong with its eyes.'

'Let me see... Oh, they're really irritated. You need to wash them with camomile water.'

He prepared the water himself and changed the cup several times until it became lukewarm. I wiped the bird with a wet gauze. It still trembled. It didn't want to eat, and I put it back in the box. After that, I started tickling it on the neck in an effort to calm it down.

'André...' my father was in the mood for talking.

'What?' I replied haughtily.

'I'd like it if we could see each other more often. Nuria and Raquel aren't around at the moment. We could...'

'I see, you're bored! Leave me alone.'

'Don't make this more difficult for me. Grandpa's death has to serve…'

'Don't talk to me about that!'

I left him with the words in his mouth and shut myself in my room. Did he need a victim in order to react?

The promises I'd made grandpa weighed like slabs of steel. I went on the Internet. My body needed to talk to Dove. I'd already added her to Messenger.

Cut Throat says:
hello, you there?
Dove says:
I thought you'd forgotten me…
Cut Throat says:
my grandpa died
Dove says:
I'm sorry, how are you?
Cut Throat says:
like a crow
Dove says:
all black?
Cut Throat says:
no, but after everything that's happened recently, I think I could fly upside down, the way it does, who knows!
Dove says:
crows are intelligent and let themselves be stroked
Cut Throat says:
they also eat prey and keep witches company in tales
Dove says:
in which case I wouldn't mind being a witch

Cut Throat says:

what are you really like?

Dove says:

it depends…

Dove says:

according to my mother, beautiful, according to the mirror, horrible

Dove says:

how do you imagine me?

Cut Throat says:

white as a dove

Dove says:

cold… I'm an Australian kind of dove, and you?

Cut Throat says:

tall, blond… a bit like Beckham

Dove says:

………………

Cut Throat says:

don't you believe me?

Dove says:

no, besides… I like them dark

Cut Throat says:

Dove says:

feeling better?

Cut Throat says:

I was never not well, didn't I tell you I'm handsome?

Dove says:

don't be bad , seriously, how are you?

> **Cut Throat says:**
> I don't know, a bit strange, I envy the eagle
> **Dove says:**
> because…?
> **Cut Throat says:**
> coz it builds its nest in faraway places and from there controls everything

I told her about the scene we'd made, first my father and then me. It helped me to talk to her. Well, I don't mean exactly 'talk', I never heard her voice.

That evening, my father tried again. He knocked at my door, I had just finished my conversation with Dove and opened. He gave me a hug, which was more like that of a little brother than a father. I let him, but didn't hug him back. At that point, he burst into tears.

'I killed him, André, I killed him,' he wet his lips with his tongue. 'Don't do the same to me.'

The weaker he appeared, the greater the rage I felt inside me. No, not rage, it was the painful, bitter taste of someone who has to gulp down a syrup for stimulating growth. He told me about Tula, who was already a little old. He then went straight into the idea that he and my mother had married too young. He was offering me his kingdom for an 'I love you', but, after being without him for so long, I'd got used to not needing him. We're better now, though he still has this obsession about being an eternal Peter Pan. I don't know if it's because he's an only child, he acts like the bird that was born first and the bird that was born last, and has ended up devouring himself.

He came out with a whole raft of good intentions. Some were too late, and I let him leave without offering a word of encouragement. All I said was, 'You were a bad father and a bad son.' 'A bad son', I felt these words like a boomerang that landed in the pit of my stomach, but I let him go without correcting myself. I then promised I would change my attitude if he came back into the room, but he didn't.

I went back to school in the last week of January. The magpie had to eat on a regular basis, and there was no one at grandma's house to make sure of that, so I decided to take it with me in a perforated box in my rucksack. I wanted to raise it myself, and my place – on its own, at the back and by the window – seemed discreet. I thought, if grandpa could do it in a boat, then I could in a classroom.

I arrived at school and whiled away the time in the toilets, until the bell for morning class rang. I'd already given it its ration of egg, cake and seeds, which I carried in an airtight container. The first problem arose in class. It was an English lesson, and everybody had sat down; if the teacher came in and you were still in the corridor, she wouldn't let you in. Our tutor had had the bright idea of moving people around. The only free place was next to Halima. I sat down and looked at her, I needed her on my side.

'Hey, I have a bird with me,' I said, pointing at the rucksack between my legs.

Her reaction unsettled me. I thought all the blood rushing to her face might force open a crack and splash all over me.

'You whaaaat?' she stuttered uncomfortably.

'I have a magpie chick in a box.'

'Ah, the one you talked about at the funeral?'

'That's right. You know…' I was silent for a moment, 'that business about grabbing a cat…'

At this point, the English teacher came in and gave us a piercing look. We both fell silent. The whole class fell silent. I was actually relieved not to have to clarify things. The magpie was similarly afraid of the teacher and behaved very well, but what happened during the natural sciences lesson was like an adventure story, I don't know whether the beginning was comic or tragic, but the ending was terribly tense. Needless to say, the natural sciences teacher hadn't turned up that day, nor had he informed of his absence, so Raúl Pernas and his gang decided to close the door so the teacher on duty wouldn't notice we were on our own.

From the music room came the notes of someone practising the flute. The tune passed straight through the wall, and the chick must have thought it was at home and started making noises that gave the game away. I stuck my hand in the box, hoping to calm it down, but somehow it quickly jumped out and on to the floor. I was so hysterical I couldn't think straight and immediately lunged at it. It immediately jumped further away, it was so frightened it didn't recognize me. The chair fell over, and the eyes of Raúl Pernas and Héctor Solla fell on me like poisoned arrows. I cowered and sat back down. The bird chirped anxiously between the desks.

'It's not mine,' I said treacherously like Judas.

'You sure, girlie?' Héctor Solla did his best to humiliate me.

The entire class went quiet. It was a rigid silence, as if we were all afraid our words might wound the air. Well, not all of us. Raúl Pernas' inflated cheeks were on the verge of bursting into a sadistic guffaw.

'I brought it,' Halima lied while getting up in an effort to recover the chick, 'I found it in front of school this morning. It was in the middle of the road and, since it can't fly…'

But Héctor Solla was quicker and grabbed it like a toy, barely letting its beak show between his fingers. I had the impression it was going to suffocate and shouted with all the forcefulness I could manage:

'Come on, give it to her!'

'Oh, look, girlie likes birds,' he carried on provoking me. 'Weren't you the tough guy that had it in him to grab a cat and wring its neck?'

I don't know what went through my head at that moment, it was like a tornado that enveloped me and carried my words whichever way it liked:

'Yeah, I like birds, so what? Just because I have a thing about them, don't believe it,' I swallowed my saliva and adopted the craziest expression I could, like in a duel in a western, 'that's another story. There's stuff that won't let me sleep, I'm warning you. Recently I've started getting up at night, going to the kitchen, grabbing the sharpest knife I can find and then heading straight for the exit with the aim of sticking the knife in the chest of whoever has hurt me at some point in my life. I have to be restrained because I'm out of my mind,' in my insides I asked whoever really knew me to forgive me for coming out with such a ludicrous story, but something told me I had to continue with my farce. 'There are times I even have to be tied with ropes until I calm down, just in case I succumb to another fit. My head is often overcome by the desire to destroy people who go about the world oppressing others,' at this point I paused for effect, like a real actor. 'Imagine what I could do to someone who's been bothering me for quite some time! And I'm not afraid of what might happen to me as a result. There's even a chance you'll find me one day lying dead in the middle of a pool of blood. If I fly off the handle…' Even I was impressed by the tone I was using.

'Cool it, mate!' I cannot forget Héctor Solla's astonished expression as he passed the bird back to Halima.

'Mate, you say?' I continued with my pretence of firmness. 'I want you to know that accepting my friendship means belonging to a high-risk group because, I'm telling you, when I fly off the handle…' Nobody could believe their eyes. The two bullies' confusion allowed me to come out of my shell. I felt myself growing as if somebody was protecting me from a secret place. 'No, listen, give it here, the bird is mine,' I addressed Halima, who was staring at me open-mouthed. 'Thanks a lot for trying to cover up for me, but it's not necessary, you know the bird is mine.'

I took it and pointed in a falsely threatening tone:

'What's said is said, don't forget it.'

I don't know what was going through everybody's head at that moment, I only remember that, for the first time, people didn't automatically side with the bullies and my voice resonated in every corner.

The natural sciences teacher suddenly came in, quickly as always when he was late, and noticed the tension in the air:

'What's this suspicious silence?'

No one dared tell him what had happened. I was running out of adrenalin when there came a few replies:

'Nothing, it's nothing.'

'It's just André put somebody in their place.'

'You what?' the teacher didn't understand.

'Nothing,' I went on, 'it's just I have a magpie chick that fell out of its nest a few days ago and I'm trying to help it. It has to be fed all the time, so I brought it here, but it's not a problem. Tomorrow I'll find somewhere else it can stay.'

Almost immediately, the church clock struck ten...

21

The church clock struck ten…

During the first months after grandpa's death, each toll of the bell sounded nostalgic, even if the bells were coming out with merry peals. I feel better now, we all feel better.

Just a few weeks ago, I was in the yard, looking after the birds, when the magpie suddenly appeared. At that point, I knew that grandma was nearby, it follows her like a dog. I sometimes think stupid things and wonder whether it's not grandpa's soul that continues among us, as in a fairy tale. For one thing, it knows how to make her laugh. When grandma is knitting, it pulls the wool out of the ball with its beak, the way the parrot from Patagonia used to, which helps heal her melancholy. In fact, she went so far as to rebuke my mother:

'What are you doing here? Don't you have something better to do?'

'How are you?'

'"How are you, how are you",' she aped my mother, 'better than you. Now get out of here!' she pretended to be angry.

'Will you really not leave all of this and come to Cantodarea?'

'Stop pestering me! Do you want me to go doolally? How am I supposed to persuade you that I'm fine? I have plenty to do and, thanks to God, I can do it. Now, both of you, go away!'

'I want to stay here!' I protested.

'That's because of the birds, but you don't live so far away.'

'What if they're attacked by magpies or sparrowhawks, then what?' I defended my position.

'Don't worry, I'll shoo them away with the broom, Andreíño. I don't want you bouncing from one house to another like a ball.'

Mother left, and I stayed to sort out the birds, not knowing whether I would end up spending the night in Pituco or Fonte do Oeste, up or down, as we say. I had a question buzzing around inside my mind and decided to ask it:

'Grandma, have you forgotten about grandpa?'

She stiffened for a moment, visibly upset by such an idea.

'Heavens above, darling! All my thoughts are about him.'

'All of them?' I answered unkindly.

'Well, not all, of course not…'

'Grandma…'

'What is it?'

'I prefer to stay where I am, and not just because of the birds.'

'What then?'

'Because of the Internet!'

'Well, blow me down!'

I preferred not to tell her what had happened the previous evening, when I was on my way to Pitanxo with my glasses in my hand. I'd just taken them off to wipe away the mist, I looked up, and a man was coming straight towards me on the pavement. He looked just like grandpa: the same walk, the same hair… He was coming towards me, and I felt my heart in my mouth. I wanted to run and embrace him, but he carried on past. I was sorry not to have put my glasses back on in time to see who it was. I sometimes feel I never even had him, he was just a beautiful dream, that's all; other times, I imagine he's at sea…

How can you go from one end to another of your life in less time than a film lasts? I'm back home already and I don't even know how I got here. What's grandma up to? Ah, with her poetic vein, recently she's been writing a lot. I wonder if she'll turn into another Rosalía de Castro. I should give it a try. I don't know, it makes me feel lazy. If there were mental recorders, I think I'd have finished the story of my life, a story that would end like this: 'I'm a stupid finch for staggering about from one end to another of my life without realizing my watch had stopped until it was midnight'.

I went to the Alameda to see if Dove was still there, but she wasn't. I waited for a couple of minutes, watching a girl. She realized I was watching her, but made no sign that she knew me. Would I muster enough courage to address her directly? 'Are you Dove?' It wasn't necessary. Her boyfriend turned up, and they left. The strange thing is I'm not sorry for my mistake, I'm actually relieved. I think I'd prefer things to stay like this, as if Dove was from another planet.

Gosh, I'm hungry! Ugh, it smells of fried fish, I'm not having any. This bread is like stone, I don't think it's from today. I'll take some sliced bread instead. Yummy, this ham is delicious! Tomatoes… where are the tomatoes?

'Grandma, I'm going to my bedroom.'

'Oh, there you are, pumpkin, I was worried.'

'I lost track of time in the Alameda.'

'Well, be sensible next time and give me a call. You said you'd be back at eleven.'

'My watch stopped, I'm not joking! Can't you see it's not working? OK, OK, don't look at me like that, I'll let you know next time, I agree. I'm going upstairs. See you tomorrow.'

'Drink a little hot milk before you go, come on.'

'Later, I have something to do.'

I owe Dove an explanation. This tastes great. If I wasn't so lazy, I'd go down and make another. Would you look at my glasses? I don't like these lenses at all, they weigh very little, but they're always getting misted up. I'd better finish this first or I'll put crumbs all over the keyboard. That was delicious! All right then. The Internet is fast now. I can't believe it, Dove is online! She's either really virtual or she doesn't live far from the Alameda... or else, of course, she just didn't turn up for our meeting.

Dove says:
I waited almost half an hour and you didn't come
Cut Throat says:
I lost track of time, I'm trying to be honest
Dove says:
you always have been, haven't you?
Cut Throat says:
I like this classmate a lot
Dove says:
I'm intrigued
Cut Throat says:
I've told you about her before
Cut Throat says:
her name is Halima...
Dove says:
and...?

Cut Throat says:
well, you wanted to meet...
Dove says:
that was so that we could see each other
Cut Throat says:
I lost track of time...
Cut Throat says:
what if we carry on like this?
Dove says:
like this, what do you mean?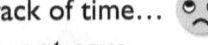
Cut Throat says:
just imagining each other...
Dove says:
 what are you afraid of?
Cut Throat says:
it's not that

If I had enough courage, I'd tell her I have a strange sensation, like I was being a traitor or something...

Dove says:
what is it then...?
Cut Throat says:
OK, maybe it is that, I don't know...

22

I don't know…

Today, I got up in a strange mood, wanting to see Halima, to open up for the birds… It's as if my body belonged to someone else. It's ten in the morning, the secretary's office has been open for more than an hour, and we must be the first people to come and collect our marks, I can't see anybody.

'Do you want me to wait for you here?'

'No… you have to come with me, otherwise they won't give them to me.'

'How much did you say we have to pay?'

'One euro.'

'So what did you break?'

'Nothing, some others broke a blind on purpose. Those in class A have to pay three euros each. The plugs turned up on the floor, and one of those large windows was smashed.'

'Well, I'm not sure it's fair that the rest of you have to pay.'

'Those are the rules, either you accuse somebody or you end up like everybody else. I wonder if the secretary is going to see us. Ah, about time!'

'Class and name?'

'9B, Santomé Lobeira, André.'

'Is this your mother?'

'Yes,' the woman must be daft, does she think it's my girlfriend?

'One euro, as you know, those in your class, one euro.'

'I know…' I wonder how my mother will react.

'Oh dear, English in the end… They're OK, I thought they might be worse. It hasn't been a good year for anyone. Maths and natural sciences are great.'

'That's because I like them more, but I'll pass English in September, I promise.'

'That's the spirit. OK, behave. I'm going now, otherwise I'll be late. What are you going to do?'

'Hang around for a while to talk to my classmates and so on.'

'Well, don't be late for grandma, you know she likes to have lunch early.'

'Yeah.'

If only Halima would come. I was great, the last day of class everybody went around exchanging phone numbers, and I shied away. I don't know what to do! I hope I'm not going to do what I did with Dove and end up waiting for no reason. I'll ask the secretary if she already came. What if she pulls my leg? She likes to talk, this one. Oh, come on. If I don't try, I'll never know. Here goes…

'Has Halima been to get her marks? She's also in 9B.'

'Halima what?'

'Atif, Halima Atif,' there was hardly going to be more than one in the school. This woman is over the top.

Oh, what a coincidence! Earth, swallow me! Here she comes with her father. I suppose it's her father. Scarper, André, scarper!

'Atif, Halima…'

Oh, for God's sake, not so loud, is this woman stupid? Why does she have to repeat the name? What shall I do?

'Yeah, that's me.'

Wow, that was lucky! She thinks the woman recognized her, but I bet she doesn't even know her own work colleagues. She's far too stuck-up.

'Hello, André!'

Lacking the capacity I thought I had as a child to disappear, I suppose I'd better answer. Come on, André, isn't this what you wanted?

'Hi, how's it going?'

The secretary must think we came together, otherwise she'd hang me out to dry. How embarrassing! She looks so pretty in pink. I'll go outside slowly, see if she comes too. Ah, here she is! Why doesn't she stop?

'Have a good summer and look after your birds.'

'Would you like to meet them?' There, I said it! Ah, I'm going to have a heart attack! 'I'd like you to witness a very special spectacle.'

'When?'

'Today, if you're not busy… I live at *The Birdhouse* with my grandma, at the upper end of Arealonga, in Pituco.'

'Yeah, I know, I've seen you heading down there,' she already knows! 'What time?'

What time shall I say? Ah, I feel so nervous!

'OK, see you this afternoon.'

'Yeah, but what time?'

'What time? Oh, five o'clock…'

'OK, see you then.'

It's ten past five. I put on the CD by Ángel González and Pedro Guerra. I did it deliberately, the birds also like voices that are caressed by a guitar: 'And it took us to a strange place we would never come back from…' The sun is still beating down on the yard. I'm exhausted from so much cleaning, but I don't want her to notice when she arrives. What's Luísa doing? OK, she decided right now to hang the washing out on the line, can't she see she's in the way?

'I'm going to show the birds to a friend of mine…' let's see if she gets the message.

That's it, she's leaving now. Hey, what's she doing back?

'André, there's a girl here who says you have a meeting.'

What a cheek! Didn't I just tell her so? What's that naughty gesture for? Halima will see her. At last, she understood, I thought she'd never go!

'It looks like a nature park!'

Great, she likes it. How big her eyes are!

Caco, as usual when a stranger turns up, has hidden. Roque's jumping all around her like he's known her all his life. I wish I had his daring!

'Come here, Roque! He oversteps himself. He's being nice to me because he knows he did something bad.'

'What did he do?'

How lovely her laugh is!

'A small blackbird, a chick, it was learning how to fly, but, because Roque was chasing it, it became frightened and couldn't move its wings. It hid in a hole in the wall. I was watching, but the only thing I could do was shout, "Be still now, be still now!" But it didn't help. The dog went mad, he lost his mind. I can still hear him whining. Another blackbird turned up, screeching loudly, even confronting Roque. It was the mother, but there was nothing it could do. Roque took the chick out of the wall with his paw and crushed it. I punished him, but I'm still not sure he's learned his lesson. These dogs are not very sharp. See? That's Caco, he's a disaster, far too fearful. If I don't call him, he won't come over and, if somebody opens the door, he'll go and hide. The only thing they've learned is not to enter the restaurant.'

'Here, Caco! Here, boy!'

Would you look at him respond to her! Here he comes. Now he won't let go of her hand. He likes being stroked. I wouldn't mind being Caco for a while. Roque's always so jealous, here he comes, behind the other two, waiting for his turn. I should say something, it's not good to be so quiet. I don't know why I'm so… I don't know… like this, as if my stomach was too full and about to burst, even though I almost haven't eaten today.

'This small one's dumb as well, he learned from the big one. He was left as a pup in a box in front of the bar, grandpa felt sorry for him and took him in. That said, when it comes to sheltering dogs, there's nobody like a friend of mine. Any stray dog he finds he takes home with him.'

'Hello there! Hey, that tickles, it almost pecked my finger! There are lots of them!'

'They were left me by my grandpa Guillerme.'

'And who are you going to leave them to?'

'I don't know, they might be happier if I let them go,' don't look at me like that, what eyes! 'But if you let them go in winter, they die. Now's a good time, there are seeds and crops… Even so, I'm a little afraid. It used to be grandpa who looked after that side of things, he knew exactly when to do it.'

'They say they have an instinct that warns them of danger.'

'That's right. Whenever the sparrowhawk's about, it's incredible, without ever having seen it before, some of them die of a heart attack, others stick their legs up in the air.'

'They sense danger better than humans.'

'I suppose so. See? If I let them go, they'll go after those cabbage pods,' hmmm! She smells like the notes of a harmonica. 'Those small pods that appear after the flower, they need to have something to eat. The trouble is lots of them eat millet and seeds we don't have,' what shall I do? Perhaps I should take her hand or kiss her. 'My grandpa put this old fridge here. We always have something, lettuce, apples… At times, they eat more of one thing or another, it all depends. When there's nothing else, I go out into the fields for mustards. To begin with, the neighbours used to make fun of me, they laughed at me for collecting herbs no one else wanted, they thought I was going to study them,' if only I was sure she liked me…

'It's strange, I'm here for the first time, and it's like I've been here before.'

'That happens to me as well, I go somewhere I've never been before, and it's like I've been there before. Perhaps it's true our dreams go ahead of us,' what nonsense I'm talking!

'Perhaps we transmigrate.'

She has such a lovely laugh.

'Who knows?'

She's so pretty, what if I try…? No, I don't even dare touch her, though my hands want to go towards her.

'Hey, don't cling to the wire like that, you're frightening me. What are those ones?'

'Those ones up there are linnets, and those down there are finches. See that one with a brown back and orange around its head? In winter, it loses all its colour and turns chestnut. And that one, see? That yellow one turns grey like a sparrow. We used to have turtledoves…'

'They say that turtledoves are loyal to their partner until they die.'

'It depends, if you put two of them on their own in a cage, yes, but if they have lots of temptations and plenty to choose from…'

'In order to be faithful, would you need to be put in a cage?'

'I'm not sure, we cut throats are pretty faithful,' I can feel the blood rushing to my ears. 'Cut throats are finches, those grey ones, see them?'

'The ones with red feathers around their neck, like your necklace…'

'Yeah, they look like their neck has been cut. That one there's not very well, see? It's all huddled up and doesn't chirp at all. That's how my grandpa ended up, without complaining.'

I swear the bit about my grandfather came out without my thinking, I didn't do it so she would kiss me on the face. Now how do I react? I feel my soul is inflamed, like it was spitting out fire.

'You remember that story we read in Galician, about a boy who spent his time trapping butterflies in his mouth?'

Why did I say that? Now look where I've got to! What's she going to think? I can hardly take it back.

'It was nice.'

'Yeah, it was cool, especially when the girl agreed to share the game with him,' oh, I'm getting braver!

It's just I don't know what to talk about, I can't think of anything. It's as if my brain and my lungs have been emptied, I'm suffocating!

'Do they know you?'

Oof! Thank goodness she changed the subject.

'Sure they do. Wait there for a minute. I'll go in, and you'll see,' now I whistle, and she can watch them approach. 'Wait a minute, I'll give them something to eat,' that's right, here you come, here you come… 'Hey, stop tickling me!'

'You'd make a good photo! But how do you get out without them following you?'

'Two claps, and they leg it. They're trained, like in the circus. Do you want to come in?'

'OK then. Hey, they've all flown away! This is obviously not my thing.'

'Not at all. They don't know you, but they'll come back. Just wait. Open your hands, and I'll give you a little birdseed. That's enough. Now stay still, don't move, and you'll see how they come to you,' I'd never noticed her hands, they're slim, I like them, but I'm not going to tell her. Enough of those heartbeats! They're making my whole body shake. 'Stay calm!' I'm the one who should stay calm.

'I must look like a real scarecrow, with my arms out like this!'

'Shhh, don't talk! They're used to me, but you shouldn't talk until they know you. Apparently, during courtship, the males shower the females with gifts, they sing to them and dance seductively. Some even leave flowers in the nest,' now why did I say that?

'That's right! I read in a book that the bowerbird, I think it is, puts an orchid in the nest.'

'And even when the female's still incubating, the male brings her food; and, if she goes out to drink, he takes care of the eggs and carefully moves them so the heat will cover them all over, just as she does.'

How pretty she is like that, with her eyelids pressed tight, like someone waiting for a surprise attack! I use this moment, as the Galician teacher would say, to 'rediscover the wonderful landscape of her anatomy'. The sun, beating on her hair, gives it a varnish finish. Here comes a canary! Clever thing! It lands straight on her hair.

'Aahhh!'

'Stay calm, it's just a canary. Let it discover you. Don't close your hands. You can open your eyes if you want to!'

'I feel a little bit cornered.'

Her laughter climbs into the air like birdsong. Her voice is nice even when she whispers. I like listening to her with my eyes! Would you look at that good-for-nothing use this opportunity to land on her chest. There he goes, jumping down. That's it, you monkey, you just pretend.

'Stay still, it's studying you, it must think you're a new species of tree.'

Here comes a parakeet, that goes straight to her hand. And another…

'Talk softly to them, so they don't go away.'

'Hello, my name is Halima Atif. I would like to fly to Chaouen on the wings of some of you,' I wouldn't mind being that bird. 'That's where I was born, in between two giants, the mountains Tisuka and Megu, near the fountain of Ras El Ma. All I remember are the narrow streets, the white and blue houses, the clean air, the washing places, the mills… I don't know if you birds are interested in any of that…'

'They're a little rude, you just carry on.'

What shall I do? How can I conquer her soul? 'Slowly like someone following a river on foot', grandpa knew how…

'I remember the music of the water playing with the stones,' I'm going to fill her hands with seed again so they don't go away, I want to carry on watching her. 'What else shall I say?' What if I say, 'Did I ever tell you you have very pretty hands.' 'My mother fell ill, and we had to move to Ouezzane. From Ouezzane, I remember the smell of olives, the vast height of the old Zaniya minaret, which I wanted to climb so I could contemplate the universe. Let's see. I remember the taste of the figs, of the deliciously sweet couscous my aunt Chislan used to make… Oh, André, my arms are getting tired!'

'Stay still! Ah, they've flown away!'

'Don't worry, I've had the sensation of talking to them, it was amazing. When are you going to let them go? I'd like to be here, watch them take flight…'

'Today's a good day. Come on, open up!'

'Now? Really?'

'Of course, open up!'

'There you go!'

'Come here, get out of the way, otherwise they won't come out. Roque, get out of here! Caco, you leave as well. I don't trust you, and nor do the birds, can't you see they won't come out? Come on, the sky is yours! Go and become independent, off you go!'

'They don't want to come out!'

'Yes, they do… There goes the first one! It's a robin. Look, look, those are canaries. There are two serins, those, those are blackbirds…'

'Hey, they're all leaving! I can't even count them any more!'

'The sky is filling up with black dots, how nice!'

'André, it's the phone for you!'

Damn, I thought grandma wasn't at home.

'Who is it, grandma?'

'Curro, he says he has something very urgent to tell you.'

Curro? What does he want?

'It's a friend, I'll be back soon.'

Unbelievable! How embarrassing! How come I didn't realize sooner? Now I understand… Even if I try to pretend, she's going to notice.

'Did something happen to your friend?'

'Well, no, not exactly.'

'It's just the colour of your face has changed. If I'm in the way, I'll leave.'

'No! It's just that Curro is a friend, a friend I need to clear up a few things with, and he's just deciphered a message I gave him.'

'A message?'

'That's right… The point is I wasn't expecting it, and I'm a little surprised, I had no idea…' I'm going to tell her outright! 'How long have you known that Cut Throat…'

'You're not talking about the note I wrote you in Arabic…?'

'Well, yes…'

'Are you disappointed? When you read out that story in social sciences, I immediately knew it was you.'

What a joke!

'It's just I imagined you…'

'White? You imagined me white? I already told you I'm an Australian kind of dove, the imperial pigeon, I like dressing in lots of colours.'

'Today, you're in pink,' what nonsense I'm talking!

'That's because today… I'm a dove from Mauritius!'

I love it when she looks at me like that, slowly, her face like a bunch of red roses. Perhaps I'm dead and already in heaven. I feel strange. I'd even like her to leave so I had an excuse to kiss her.

'Come, lie like this on the ground, it's amazing watching them…'

And here we are, the two of us lying on the grass, holding hands, Dove and Cut Throat, just as the note in Arabic said. Two butterflies fly overhead like two sparks…

The CD carries on playing:

… around here a river passes by,
around here your footsteps
have beautified the sand
and cleared the water…

'Do you know what I would like to be called?'

'What?'

'Garuda.'

'Garuda? Sounds good…'

Read more titles in the series published by Small Stations Press!

Agustín Fernández Paz, BLACK AIR

Had I remained silent, had I concealed my interest at that point, I might now be in a completely different situation, far away from the horror that has been ceaselessly gnawing away at me for the past three years. And yet my words simply paved the way for what Dr Montenegro had to say:

'You will learn more about Laura Novo, Dr Moldes. She is going to be your first patient. Under my supervision, of course. You have new ideas, you may be the only person capable of shedding light on a case that has kept the rest of us in the dark. I know it's not an easy challenge, but perhaps, with your passion for knowledge, you're the only one who can find a solution that goes beyond the boundaries of accepted practice. I'll have her case history sent to you at once. Good luck, Víctor, my friend, and welcome to Beira Verde Clinic!'

Víctor Moldes is an outstanding psychiatry student, looking to test his knowledge on patients. He is given a job at the prestigious Beira Verde Clinic in Galicia, near the Portuguese border, and handed a patient, Laura Novo, who is capable only of writing her name on blank sheets of paper. Slowly he draws her out of herself and she agrees to tell him her story, how she left Madrid in order to work on her thesis and escape a difficult relationship that was going nowhere. Her return to the land where she grew up, to stay in a guest house run by a schoolteacher she had fallen passionately in love with when she was a teenager, has fatal consequences. Her presence in the remote area of Terra Chá awakens the Great Beast, who up until that moment had been slumbering in the depths of the earth. Once awake, the Great Beast has one year to achieve its objective. Dr Moldes finds himself drawn into a conflict he is barely able to understand, let alone control, and, having finally pieced together the fragments of the narrative, he is in a race against time to save his patient.

ISBN 978-954-384-028-1

'The night is a lot more alive. You can see colours better than during the day,' Vincent had told me.

Adeline and I, sitting on the ground very close to each other, watched him paint under the moonlight. He had a small candle attached to the brim of his hat and had placed two bigger candles on the easel to illuminate the canvas, where he was releasing brushstrokes with the same burning enthusiasm as always.

I was afraid at some stage the wax might melt and Vincent would burn himself or cause a fire in the field where we were sitting, but he carried on talking and painting without a rest. I still couldn't believe I was there in Adeline's company, alone under the night sky, surrounded by sheaves of wheat.

When Vincent told me he planned to go on a nocturnal expedition, I was very surprised.

A teenage boy is sent by his mother to spend a few days in the country as a way of getting him out of trouble. In the town of Auvers-sur-Oise, one hour north of Paris, the boy finds life with his great-aunt unbearable — that is until the arrival of the painter Vincent van Gogh, who has come to escape difficulties in the south. It is the summer of 1890 and already eight months have passed since the boy left his mother. He begins a friendship with the painter, taking him to places he hasn't seen and engaging in conversations that open his eyes to a different way of viewing the world, bringing to an end his turbulent past. He also struggles with the reasons for his mother's disappearance from the town where she grew up and experiences the first embers of romantic love when he develops an interest in the daughter of van Gogh's innkeeper, Adeline. Based on real events, this imaginative story of a teenage boy's friendship with an inspired painter and participation in the events of a provincial town, where he meets the local doctor, a war hero, and railway pointsman, as well as the man who could turn out to be his real father, rushes to its inevitable conclusion like the trains that slice through the countryside on their way to Paris.

ISBN 978-954-384-030-4

Elena Gallego Abad, DRAGAL I: THE DRAGON'S INHERITANCE

'Have a look around you, with wide open eyes. The catacombs are not far from here, but you have to be the one to find the keys. I shan't be able to accompany you on the last stage of your journey, I'm getting too old for such adventures, so I must fulfil my role as guide by getting you to come up with the correct answers. When it's time, the result will depend on your choices. And don't forget the search for the dragon will be worthless if you lose what matters to you most along the way.'

The priest spoke slowly and the boy began to feel desperate. Father Xurxo didn't seem prepared to give him the indications he needed and impatience was gnawing away at his soul.

'Please…'

The vicar took an apple out of his pocket, wiped it on the sleeve of his jacket and sat on a pew in the first row, gesturing to the boy to sit down beside him.

'Have a look around you, with wide open eyes, and tell me what you see,' he said again, biting into the fruit.

After the death of his father in a caving accident, Hadrián is forced to move to Galicia with his mother and start at a new school. His mother gives him a medallion that belonged to his father, showing a dragon in a threatening posture on one side and the same dragon incubating an egg on the other. When the dragon's tails move, the boy realizes this is no ordinary medallion. Meanwhile, he has noticed the stone effigy of a dragon on the cornice of St Peter's Church, which winks at him and infiltrates his thoughts. The boy's destiny, it seems, is to sacrifice himself so that the dragon can come back to life after an interval of a thousand years, during which it has been protected in the catacombs under the church. The boy and his classmate Mónica will first have to locate the catacombs with the help of the parish priest, Father Xurxo, before they can ascertain whether the dragon's existence is for real.

ISBN 978-954-384-031-1

Read more Galician literature in English published by Small Stations Press!

Fiction:

Álvaro Cunqueiro, FOLKS FROM HERE AND THERE

Poetry:

Manuel Rivas, FROM UNKNOWN TO UNKNOWN

Lois Pereiro, COLLECTED POEMS

Celso Emilio Ferreiro, LONG NIGHT OF STONE

Rosalía de Castro, GALICIAN SONGS

Pilar Pallarés, A LEOPARD AM I

Xosé María Díaz Castro, HALOS

For an up-to-date list of our publications, please visit www.smallstations.com

For more information on Galician literature in English, please visit www.galicianliterature.com